THE GREAT BIG BOOK
SPACE

PETER GREGO

**Australian
GEOGRAPHIC**

Copyright © 2009 QED Publishing

First published in the UK in 2009 by
QED Publishing
A Quarto Group Company
The Old Brewery, 6 Blundell Street
London N7 9BH

www.qed-publishing.co.uk

Author Peter Grego
Produced by Calcium
Editor Sarah Eason
Illustrations by Geoff Ward
Picture Researcher Maria Joannou

Printed in China

Published by Australian Geographic
An imprint of Bauer Media Ltd
54 Park Street, Sydney, NSW 2000
Telephone +61 2 9263 9813
Email education@ausgeo.com.au
www.australiangeographic.com.au

Australian Geographic customer service
1300 555 176 (local call rate within Australia)
+61 2 8667 5295 outside Australia

This edition published by
Australian Geographic in 2014
Copyright © 2009 QED Publishing

ISBN: 9781742451275

Words in **bold** can be found in the
glossary on page 112.

Picture credits
Key: T = top, B = bottom, C = centre, L = left, R = right,
FC = front cover, BC = back cover

Alamy Images/Visual Arts Library (London) 10
Jamie Cooper 101T
Corbis /Bettmann 72, /Tom Bean 80–81, /Jonathan Blair
78–79, / Jim Craigmyle 29B, /Ric Ergenbright 82–83, Eugen/
Zefa 35, /Firefly Productions 28–29, /Simon Marcus 8, /
NASA 34–35, /David Muench 79B /Roger Ressmeyer 10–11,
26–27, 29T, 91B, /Howard Sochurek 18BL, /Ute & Juergen
Schimmelpfennig/Zefa 93B /Visuals Unlimited 18BR /Robert
Weight/Ecoscene 37T
CTIO/NOAO/AURA/NSF 33B
ESA 57T
Getty Images /Amana 40B, /Hulton Archive 12, /Iconica
37B, Iconica FCB, 67B, /Imagebank 76–77, /Photodisc, 90,
94–95, 96, /Photodisc FCB, 6–7, 12, 18, 57B, 87T /Photo-
disc FCT, FCC, 34, 38, 46, 49T, 59B, /Photodisc FCT, 62, BC,
/Taxi 72–73
Peter Grego 13, 17B, 18TL, 23T, 53B
Istockphoto/Dar Yang Yan 19
NASA FCT, FCC, 1, 3, 16–17, 18TR, 21T, 24–25, 24, 29,
31, 36, 39B, 43B, 45T, 45B, 47T, 47B, 49B, 51B, 52, 55T,
55B, 56, 60, BC, 65B, 66, 74, 75B, /GSFC 75T, 86, 87B,
88, 88–89, 89, 95B, 98, 99B, 99T, 100B, 101B, 102, 103T,
104, 105B, 105T, 106, 107T, 109T, 110, 111B, BC, /CXC/M.
Markevitch et al 15B, /Neil A. Armstrong 107B, ESA 23B, /
ESA/SOHO 7B, 18LM, /ESA/M. Robberto and the Hubble
Space Telescope Orion Treasury Project Team 32,/GSFC/
Jacques Descloitres/MODIS Rapid Response Team 68–69,
/GSFC/Craig Mayhew and Robert Simmon 84–85, /The
Hubble Heritage Team (STScI/AURA) 54, /JPL 39T, 40T, 41,
42–43, 43T, /JPL-Caltech 51T /JPL-Caltech 33T /Hubble Her-
itage 5B, 9B, 22–23, 25, /Hubble Heritage Team/STScI/AURA
27T, /IKONOS 3, /JPL-Caltech 64, /JPL 92, /JPL-Caltech 93T,/
JPL-Caltech/STScI 15T, /JPL-Caltech/ Univ. of Ariz 14–15, /
Kennedy Space Center 103B, /Harrison H. Schmitt FCC, 108,
/USGS 70, 71T
NGDC 85
NOAA 83, 84, /Lieutenant Philip Hall 69;
Rex Features 111t Sipa Press;
Science Photo Library 54, /Chris Butler 82, /Celestial Im-
age Co 20–21, /Russell Croman 97, 100T, /Mark Garlick 48,
63T, FCB, /David A Hardy 19, 65T, /Harvard College Ob-
servatory 61,/Magrath Photography 12–13, Library /NASA
52–53, /NASA/ESA/STSCI/Erich Karkoschka/University of
Arizona 58, /Walter Pacholka/Astropics 67T, /Emilio Segre/
Visual Archives/ American Institute of Physics 17T, /John San-
ford 95T /Soames Summerhays FCC, /Dirk Wiersma 79T /
Sheila Terry 59T, /Detlev Van Ravenswaay 60–61; Wikipedia
Commons Public Domain 31
Nik Szymanek 27B
USGS 80, 81, /Seth Moran 77.

Website information is correct at time of going
to press. However, the publisher cannot accept
liability for any information or links found on
third-party websites.

CONTENTS

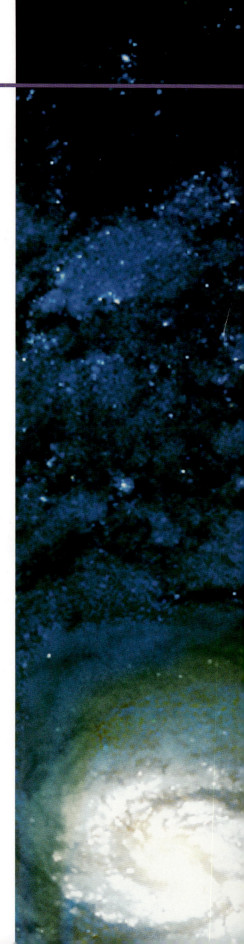

VOYAGE THROUGH EARTH

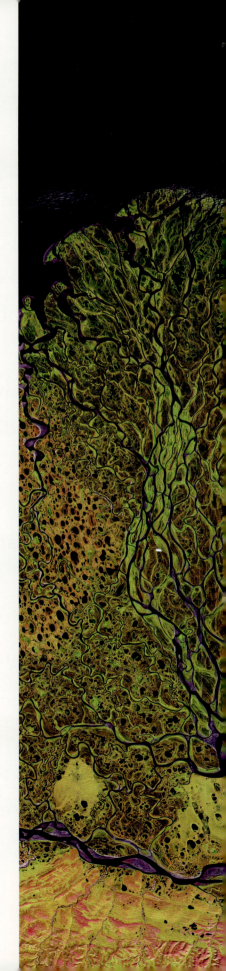

DISCOVERING THE MOON

INTRODUCING THE UNIVERSE

Everything there is makes up the **universe**. Our own home in the universe, the **planet** Earth, looks very big to us. But when we look at it from **space**, we realize it is only a ball of rock, one of eight planets circling around a **star** called the sun.

Our sun is actually a star. Like all stars, it is an incredibly hot ball of gas. It is so big that more than a million Earths could fit inside it. Now our Earth doesn't seem so big, does it? The sun and the planets and their moons, together with millions of chunks of ice, dust and gases called **comets** and thousands of lumps of rock called **asteroids**, make up our **solar system**.

⇧ Stars are formed in huge clouds of gas and dust.

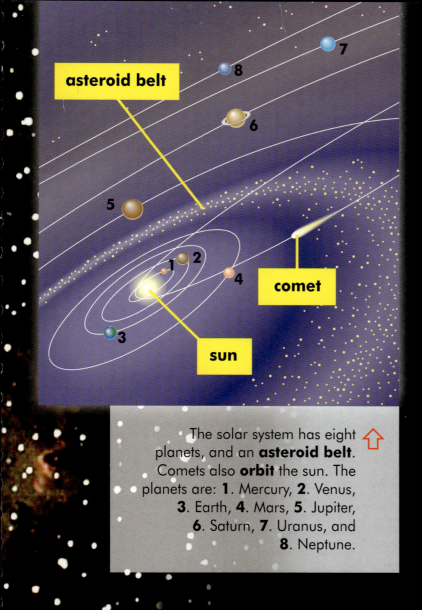

asteroid belt

7

8

6

5

1 2

4

comet

3

sun

The solar system has eight planets, and an **asteroid belt**. Comets also **orbit** the sun. The planets are: **1**. Mercury, **2**. Venus, **3**. Earth, **4**. Mars, **5**. Jupiter, **6**. Saturn, **7**. Uranus, and **8**. Neptune.

A galaxy of stars

The stars we can see from Earth look small and faint because they are amazingly far away. They lie outside our solar system and may be bigger or smaller, hotter or cooler, older or younger than our sun. Many may have their own solar systems, too. All the stars we can see in the night sky belong to a vast **galaxy** called the **Milky Way**. This is a spiral galaxy that is shaped like a fried egg, thick at the centre and thinner on the outside.

A colossal universe

The Milky Way is unimaginably big, but it is only a very tiny part of the universe. There are billions more galaxies in the universe, some shaped like spirals, others like gigantic footballs.

The Whirlpool Galaxy, photographed by the Hubble Space **Telescope** – an enormous telescope that orbits Earth.

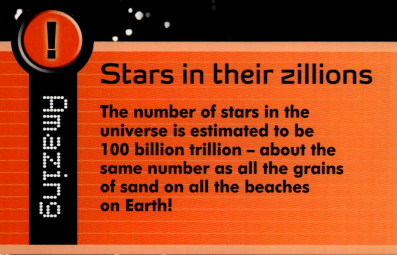

Amazing

Stars in their zillions

The number of stars in the universe is estimated to be 100 billion trillion – about the same number as all the grains of sand on all the beaches on Earth!

UNIVERSAL FORCES

A few basic forces are in control of the universe. A force called **gravity** pulls little objects toward bigger objects. For example, when a ripe apple falls off a tree on Earth, gravity pulls it towards Earth's surface and makes it hit the ground.

When you throw a ball into the air, gravity pulls it down again. If you could throw the ball hard enough, it would climb so high that it would become a little moon in orbit around Earth.

Let's play ball with gravity

The next time you are playing ball on a warm, sunny day, remember that you owe your fun to the laws of the universe. Invisible powers are at work! You cannot see gravity, but it is the force that makes your ball curve through the air and fall back to the ground at a certain speed. Earth's gravity also acts on the **moon**, making it circle around us. The moon travels once around Earth each month. Gravity also makes Earth orbit the sun in an oval. It makes one complete lap in a year. Planet Mars is smaller than Earth and has just one-third of its gravity. There, because the force of gravity is weaker than on Earth, a ball will fly three times further when it is hit with the same force. Sports rules will need to be different when people play ball on Mars!

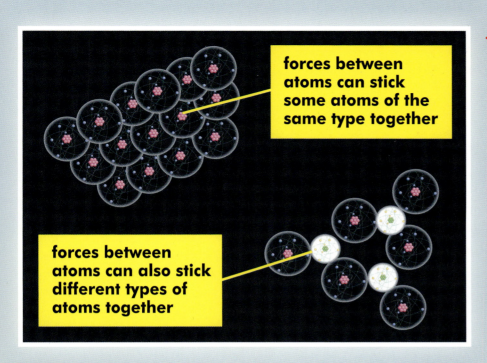

forces between atoms can stick some atoms of the same type together

forces between atoms can also stick different types of atoms together

Tiny particles called **atoms** are the smallest pieces of matter. Forces inside atoms hold them together. These forces can stick some atoms of the same type together or stick atoms of different types together to form **molecules**.

Atoms make up everything in the universe. They are like tiny building blocks.

Key Concept

Radiation

Radiation is any kind of energy in the form of rays, waves or energetic particles that travel through the air or another substance. Light is a type of radiation that we can see, and heat is a form of radiation that we can feel. Other types need special equipment to be detected. The sun gives off a lot of light and heat, as well as other types of radiation.

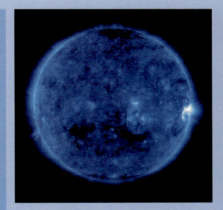
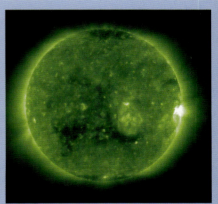
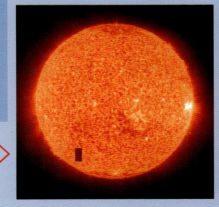
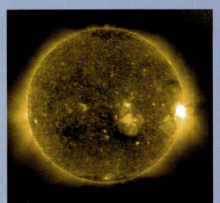

These four pictures of the sun show different radiation temperatures in the sun's **atmosphere**. They were taken by an **observatory** in space called SOHO, which studies the sun.

AN EARTH-CENTRED UNIVERSE

A philosopher is someone who thinks about problems and tries to solve them. In Ancient Greece, philosophers thought a lot about the universe. They were on the right track about many things because they were very good at maths, which can be used to find out how the universe works.

About 2250 years ago, a philosopher called Aristarchus worked out how big Earth was. He also made a pretty good estimate of the distances from Earth to the moon and to the sun. He said, correctly, that Earth spins around each day while it orbits the sun. People did not like this idea. They preferred to believe another philosopher, Aristotle, who said that Earth was at the center of the universe. Aristotle said that the moon, sun, planets and stars all move around Earth at different speeds. People believed this for a very long time, until the telescope was invented in the early 17th century and Aristarchus was proved right.

Aristotle (384–322 BCE) was one of the greatest of Ancient Greek philosophers, but he was wrong about the Universe.

Orion the Hunter is an ancient constellation. It is easy to recognize in the dark evening skies of winter and spring by the three bright stars that make up Orion's belt.

Orion's belt

Constellations

Many ancient philosophers believed that the stars were attached to a giant circle surrounding Earth. People believed they saw **constellations** of gods and monsters, heroes and villains, among the patterns of these stars. To our eyes, the stars look fixed in space. However, they are actually moving, but they appear fixed because they are so far away. Their movements can be picked up by measurements made by telescopes. Incredibly, an ancient Greek would find that today's constellations look almost the same as those seen more than 2000 years ago.

Key Concept

What is a theory?

Scientists use theories to explain the workings of the universe. But a theory is not just an idea on its own. It fits in with what has been observed, and it can be tested and used to predict how things might happen in the future.

THE SUN TAKES CENTRE STAGE

About 500 years ago, when most people still believed Earth was at the centre of the universe, astronomer Nicolaus Copernicus (1473–1543) wrote a book stating similar ideas to those held by Aristarchus, 2000 years before him. Copernicus said that the sun was at the centre of the universe and Earth was a planet that orbited it. His book upset a lot of people, but it made some people think more scientifically about the universe, and the modern science of **astronomy** was born.

Biography

Galileo Galilei (1564–1642) and his eye-opening discoveries

More than 50 years after Copernicus's book was published, an Italian scientist named Galileo Galilei turned his small, homemade telescope towards the sky. He saw many things that proved Copernicus was right: Earth really was a planet orbiting the sun, just like Mercury, Venus, Mars, Jupiter and Saturn (Uranus and Neptune had yet to be discovered).

Proof that Earth really could not be at the centre of everything came when Galileo saw four tiny moons circling Jupiter every night. This proved that not everything orbited Earth because Jupiter was clearly orbited by its own moons.

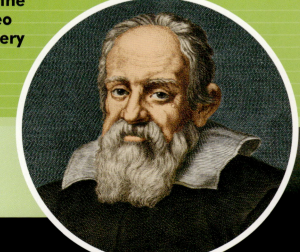

Galileo, a scientific genius, was one ⇨ of the first people to explore the universe through a telescope.

Galileo made these ink drawings of the moon from what he observed through his telescope.

Discovering the Milky Way

When Galileo looked at the misty band of the Milky Way through his telescope, he saw that it was made up of countless thousands of stars. Soon, astronomers found that these stars are spread along the flattened disk of our galaxy. We now know that the Milky Way is a spiral shape, and that our solar system lies far from its centre on one of its curving spiral arms.

The hazy band of the Milky Way can be seen from dark locations in summer. In the northern **hemisphere** it arches overhead at midnight, making a real treat for those viewing it through binoculars.

GALAXY FAMILIES

round 100 years ago, astronomers thought that the universe was only as big as the Milky Way. This idea was shattered when some faint patches of light dotted around the sky were shown to be other galaxies. They are as big as our own, but so far away that they appear small and dim through a telescope. Our ideas about the size of the universe expanded; our own Milky Way now looked rather small.

The spiral galaxy, Andromeda, is the biggest galaxy in our 'local group'.

Amazing

A near neighbour?

The Andromeda Galaxy, our 'near neighbour', is so far away that its light takes two million years to reach us!

This is the Large Cloud of Magellan, a galaxy smaller than our own, but close to us.

Our galaxy neighbours

Two large patches of light, known as the Clouds of Magellan, were found to be two small galaxies near our own. There are also other galaxies quite close by, at least on a cosmic scale. The Andromeda Galaxy, just visible from a dark location on Earth, is a spiral galaxy like the Milky Way. It is one of the Milky Way's neighbouring galaxies. The Milky Way, the Clouds of Magellan and the Andromeda Galaxy belong to a small group of around 30 galaxies that are held in place by gravity.

This distant cluster of galaxies was viewed by the Hubble Space Telescope.

Galactic superclusters

Farther away, there are many more galaxy families. These families group together to make huge galactic **superclusters**. As we look deeper into space, we peer further back in time. The Hubble Space Telescope has discovered galaxies so far away that their light takes 13 billion years to reach us.

THE EXPANDING UNIVERSE

The whole universe is expanding. The farther away a galaxy is, the faster it appears to be moving away from us! Imagine that the galaxies are chocolate chips in a biscuit (the universe) baking in the oven. As the mixture heats up, it expands and each chip, or galaxy, moves away from the others. This is how the universe expands.

Named after astronomer Edwin Hubble, the Hubble Space Telescope has viewed the universe in great detail since it was launched in 1990.

Edwin Hubble (1889–1953) and the expanding universe

In the 1920s, an American astronomer named Edwin Hubble noticed that light from distant galaxies is 'stretched' in an odd way. He realized that the light is being stretched because the galaxies are rushing away from us at enormous speeds.

⇩ Edwin Hubble is shown here with a picture of a galaxy.

The Big Bang

Hubble discovered that galaxies are rushing away from each other at incredible speeds. But, why is this happening? Astronomers now think that it is the result of an unimaginably hot and powerful 'explosion' that happened around 14 billion years ago. This explosion is called the **Big Bang**. Most scientists believe that the universe was created by the Big Bang. The galaxies are still speeding away as a result of this huge explosion.

This picture shows what the Big Bang may have looked like. ⇨

THE COSMIC CALENDAR

The universe is unimaginably old. To help us understand the stages in its life so far, let's pretend that its entire 14 billion years are squeezed into a single year. Imagine that the Big Bang occurred and the universe was created at the very start of 1st January, and the moment you are reading this is midnight on 31st December. Each month of our special cosmic year is just over one billion years long. Each week is about 270 million years long, and each day is 38 million years long.

A long year

You might be surprised to learn that our sun does not begin to shine until early in August of this year. It is followed a few hours later by the formation of Earth and the other planets in our solar system. The first signs of life wait until November to appear, and the dinosaurs arrive on the scene by 24th December.

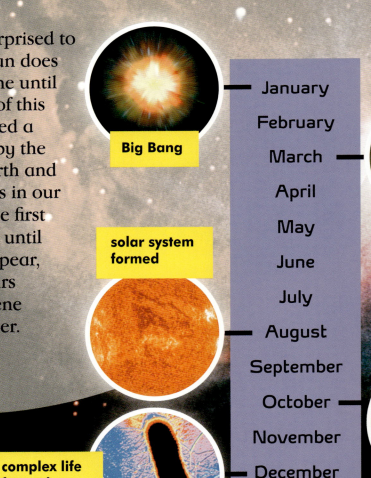

Big Bang

solar system formed

complex life formed

our galaxy formed

first life formed

January
February
March
April
May
June
July
August
September
October
November
December

December in our cosmic year

1 First complex life	8	15 New life forms flourish	22	29 Dinosaurs wiped out
2	9	16	23	30
3	10	17 First animals with backbone	24 First dinosaurs	31 Mankind
4	11	18 First land plants	25 First mammals	
5	12	19	26	
6	13	20 First animals with four limbs	27 First birds	
7	14	21 First insects	28	

Humans come along at six minutes to midnight on 31st December. The pyramids of Ancient Egypt are built in the last ten seconds of the year, and just a second before midnight, Christopher Columbus dares to voyage across the Atlantic Ocean. You are reading this book only a very small fraction of a second before midnight, on the very last day of the cosmic year!

Death of the dinosaurs

On 24th December in the cosmic calendar, the dinosaurs took their first footsteps on Earth. Just five days later, a large asteroid smashed into the planet, and most of these fantastic creatures were wiped out in a cosmic instant.

31 December
10:00
First apes

31 December
9:25 Human ancestors walk upright

9:54 First modern humans
9:59:45 Writing invented
9:59:50 Egyptian pyramids
9:59:59 Columbus visits the Americas
9.59.59.9999 You are reading this book

STARRY NIGHT

Stars are made up mainly of two gases: hydrogen and helium. These gases are so hot that the atoms that make them up move really fast. When fast-moving atoms bump into each other, they join together to make a heavier kind of atom, and a burst of energy is produced. This burst of energy, of heat and light, is what makes most stars shine.

You cannot tell how bright a star is just by looking at it because stars are at different distances from us and vary in their real brightness. A star that looks dim might be much farther away than one that looks bright.

This beautiful cluster of young stars is known as 'The Beehive'.

Star colour

Not all stars are the same colour. Some look blue, others orange. The colour of a star tells us how hot it is. Our sun is a yellow-white star. It is of medium temperature – its surface is 6,000°C. Orange or red stars are cooler than the sun, while blue stars are very much hotter.

Stars change colour during their lifetime. When they are young, they are blue; at the end of their life, they become red.

Project

How far are the stars?

Hold up a pencil and look at it with just your right eye. Now look at it with just your left eye. The pencil moved! Well, it appeared to move. This effect is called parallax, **and astronomers use it to measure distances to the stars. They note the position of a star and six months later, when Earth is on the other side of its orbit around the sun, they note its position again. The nearer the star is to us, the more it will appear to move against the distant starry background.**

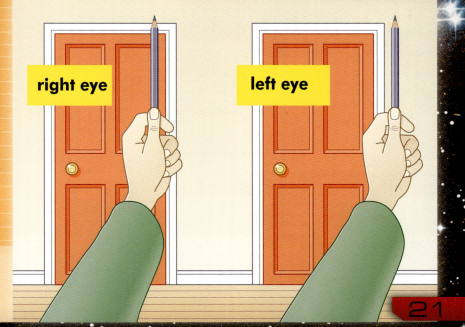

right eye

left eye

This diagram illustrates the effect of parallax.

Small stars burn up their fuel more slowly than bigger stars, so they live longer. As stars run out of fuel, they swell up and their surface cools down. Big, bloated stars like this are known as **red giants**. Eventually they puff away their gases into space. The gas and dust shells around them are called planetary nebulae ('nebulae' means 'clouds', and the shells look like little planets). The stars at the centres of planetary nebulae turn into really **dense** stars about the size of Earth. These are called **white dwarfs**.

The Helix Nebula is ⇨ one of the biggest and brightest of all planetary nebulae.

kinds of really strange objects – a **pulsar** or a **black hole**. Pulsars are small – about the size of a city – and extremely heavy. They spin up to a thousand times a second! If the star's core is squashed beyond a certain limit, it becomes a black hole. Black holes have so much gravity that everything within a certain distance is sucked into them, even light itself.

Heavy stuff

White dwarfs are so dense that a teaspoonful of their matter would weigh a ton. That's about the same as a small car. A teaspoonful of pulsar material would weigh a billion tons, which is more than all the cars in the world combined!

Amazing

This amazing image captured by the Chandra space telescope shows the remains of an exploded star in the constellation Cassiopeia.

GAS CLOUDS AND FANTASTIC FUZZIES

Inside galaxies like our own Milky Way, gigantic clouds of gas and dust stretch for tens, hundreds, even thousands of **light years** between the stars. These clouds block the light from stars behind them, so they appear as silhouettes against the starry background. If you are lucky enough to see the Milky Way at night, you will notice that it is interrupted here and there by these dark clouds.

A star is born

Inside some of the dust and gas clouds, gravity has pulled the material together to make it into dense clumps. Sometimes these become so dense that the enormous pressure and heat ignites stars within them, and the clouds surrounding the stars are lit up like beautiful lanterns. These star clouds are called nebulae and there are many wonderful examples to see in the night sky.

This nebula is called the North America Nebula because of its shape. A hot star inside it makes its gases glow.

 A cloud of dust and gas silhouetted against a bright nebula produces the shape of the famous Horsehead Nebula.

Project

The Orion Nebula

The Orion Nebula is one of the loveliest gas clouds in space. It is located just south of the well-known trio of bright stars that make up Orion's belt, and you can see it on clear winter nights and spring evenings as a small misty patch. Using binoculars or a telescope, look for wisps of gas and a dark patch of dust known as the shark's mouth. A small group of new stars shining brightly at its centre is called the trapezium.

shark's mouth

trapezium

When viewed through an ordinary telescope, nebulae do not look very colourful. But, photographs taken through big telescopes bring out their fantastic colours, with blazing blues, rippling reds and a variety of other colours.

STAR CLUSTERS

As we have seen, stars are usually born in groups inside giant clouds of gas and dust called nebulae. As time goes by, the hot wind streaming from the young stars begins to blow away the nebula around them until it disappears altogether.

Scattered across the sky are many lovely groups of young stars, some hanging on to traces of the clouds from which they were born. These star groups, known as **open clusters**, slowly get pulled apart as they travel round their galaxy. Our own sun may once have been part of a star cluster, but it was so long ago that we do not know where its original sister stars are.

Project

Seven Sisters in sight

The most famous example of a young star cluster is the Pleiades (say Ply-a-dees). This cluster is about 100 million years old. It is also known as the Seven Sisters, because people can see seven of these stars with the naked eye. Look for it on winter nights and spring evenings by following the line made by Orion's belt towards the right, by the width of about two outstretched hands.

 The bright Pleiades cluster is a close-knit collection of young, hot stars.

Globular clusters

Globular clusters are far bigger than open clusters. They contain anything from tens of thousands to millions of stars, all held together in a huge ball shape. While open clusters are made up of young stars, globular clusters contain very old, red stars, many times older than our own sun. Around 150 of these impressive clusters surround our galaxy. Other spiral galaxies are surrounded by their own globular clusters.

⬆ Globular clusters are made up of hundreds of thousands of closely packed stars, all held together in a ball shape by gravity.

This is the famous Double Cluster in the constellation Perseus. It is made up of two open clusters close together.

REVEALING THE UNIVERSE

About 400 years ago, it was discovered that glass lenses could be used in a tube to make a telescope. This could collect light and give a magnified image of a distant object, such as the moon. Ever since, astronomers have been making bigger and better lenses to collect more light and produce more detailed views of the heavens. Telescopes that use lenses to collect light are called **refractors**.

A new kind of telescope

In 1668, a brilliant scientist called Isaac Newton invented a telescope that used a mirror shaped like a shallow bowl to collect and focus light. These telescopes are known as **reflectors**. They can be built much larger than refractors, and they give a clearer image, too. Most of the world's big telescopes are reflectors, using giant mirrors to peer into the distant reaches of the universe.

⬆ The William Herschel Telescope is a reflector telescope that sits on the top of a mountain peak on La Palma in the Canary Islands.

Radio telescopes

Astronomers also use radio telescopes. These collect the radio waves from objects in space in the same way that a satellite dish on your house collects television signals. The signals the telescope collects can be used to make pictures of the objects.

With all these powerful telescopes, astronomers can reveal what is going on in deep space – from the birth of stars to matter spiraling down the funnels of black holes.

The Very Large Array in New Mexico is one of the world's most powerful radio telescopes. It consists of 27 dishes, each 25 m across.

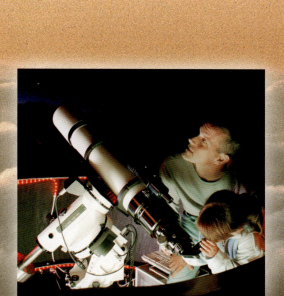

Hundreds of years ago, just a few scientists owned telescopes. Today, many people look at the universe with their own telescopes.

Telescopes are 'light buckets'

Collecting light is important to astronomers because many objects in the night sky are faint and difficult to see. The bigger a telescope's lens or mirror, the more light it can collect and the brighter and more detailed an object will appear.

Key concept

OUR COSMIC BACKYARD

Our **planet**, Earth, is one of eight planets that make up an area of **space** we call our **solar system**. Inside the solar system are our **sun** and **moon**, and the eight planets: Mars, Venus, Mercury, Earth, Jupiter, Saturn, Uranus, and Neptune. The solar system also includes the moons that orbit around some of the planets, and many comets and **asteroids**.

Mercury

sun

Mars

The four inner planets

The four planets nearest the sun are Mercury, Venus, Earth and Mars. These are called the four 'inner planets'. Each has a solid surface and, except Mercury, is surrounded by an **atmosphere**. Only Earth's atmosphere is suitable for us to breathe.

The four outer planets

The four 'outer planets' are Jupiter, Saturn, Uranus and Neptune. These are giant balls of mainly **hydrogen** and **helium** gas and are the planets farthest from the sun.

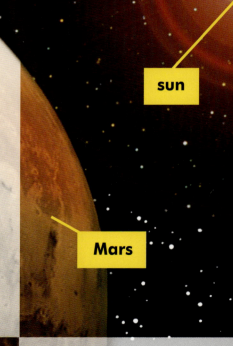

The four inner planets of ⬆ our solar system: Mercury, Venus, Earth and Mars.

The dwarf planets

As well as the eight major planets, a few smaller solid balls orbit the sun. These are called '**dwarf planets**'. They include the largest asteroid, Ceres, and the frozen worlds of Pluto and Eris.

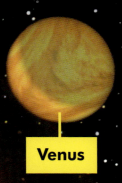

Venus

Biography

Johannes Kepler (1571–1630) and his planetary laws

Four hundred years ago, the German astronomer **Johannes Kepler figured out that all planets in the solar system travel around, or orbit, the sun in an oval-shaped path called an 'ellipse'. The nearer a planet moves towards the sun, the faster it travels. As the planet moves away from the sun, it slows down. This rule is the same for all orbiting objects – a moon orbiting a planet or a comet orbiting the sun.**

⇐ Johannes Kepler.

Comets

Comets are mountain-sized, dirty snowballs. They are mainly found in the far reaches of space, at great distances from the sun. Whenever their orbit takes them close to the sun, they heat up and throw off clouds of dust and **gas.**

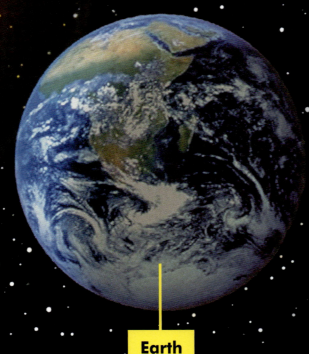

Earth

Around 4.6 billion years ago, scientists believe that something amazing happened in our **galaxy**, the Milky Way. A star exploded, sending a ripple through a large cloud of nearby dust and gas. The ripple squashed the cloud together, making it thicker in parts.

Gravity pulled on the thicker areas, which collapsed in on themselves. As the cloud collapsed, it began to spin faster and faster. This made it become flatter, thinner and cooler towards the edges, and hotter at its centre. Clumps of material in the cloud then began to stick together. As these areas became larger, gravity caused them to attract other clumps of material. The clumps of material became bigger and bigger, and eventually grew into the planets, moons, asteroids and comets that make up our solar system.

 The sun was born inside a big cloud of gas and dust, called a nebula.

Birth of the sun

The temperature at the centre of the collapsing Milky Way gas cloud became so high that it caused a huge reaction, called a **nuclear reaction**. This created the sun.

The incredible heat and energy made by the newborn sun cleared away the gases and ice in the inner part of the solar system. In this gas- and ice-free area are the four solid inner planets. Gas and ice remained in the outer system, which is where the four outer planets (made of gas) are found. The very edge of the solar system is still freezing and here millions of icy comets exist.

⇧ The young sun was surrounded by clouds of dust and gas, which clumped together to create the planets.

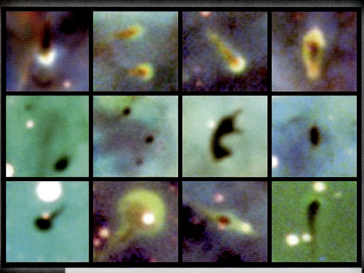

⇧ This collection of odd looking objects was found in the Carina Nebula (within the Milky Way) by a very powerful **telescope** called the Hubble Space Telescope. Each one is thought to be a very young solar system in the making.

OUR SUN, THE NEAREST STAR

The sun is a star that shines in the same way as any other star – by changing its hydrogen gas to helium gas, which makes light and heat. The sun is an enormous ball made up of mainly hydrogen gas, which is found throughout the **universe**. The sun is incredibly hot – in fact, the **pressure** and heat at the centre of the sun is a hundred thousand times hotter than your oven!

hurricane

All weather on Earth is driven by the sun's heat.

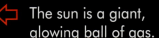
The sun is a giant, glowing ball of gas.

All plant and animal life on Earth depends upon energy from the sun.

Slowly dying

The sun provides Earth with heat and light, which drives our planet's weather and allows life to exist. If the sun were somehow switched off, our planet would become a frozen ball upon which only the simplest life forms could survive.

During the last 4.6 billion years, the sun has been slowly using up its hydrogen gas, which fuels its heat. The sun is now about halfway through its life. Eventually, in the distant future, it will use up all of its fuel and die.

Amazing

Burning up energy

Every second, the sun loses four million tons of its weight as it burns up the gas at its centre. Despite this, the sun will carry on shining for several billion more years.

SOLAR SPECTACLES

Astronomers use special telescopes to look at a very hot area above the sun's surface. Here, they can see gigantic flames of hot gases, called **solar** flares and prominences. Sunspots can also be seen on the sun's surface. These are dark spots that are actually very hot and bright, but seem dark because the rest of the sun's surface is even hotter and brighter. Sunspots are caused when hot gases flow around **magnetic fields** on the sun's surface, leaving a slightly cooler, darker-looking central area.

Warning!

Never look directly at the sun with your eyes, and never use binoculars or a telescope to view it. Raw sunlight can damage your eyes and could even make you blind. Astronomers study the sun safely using special telescopes and equipment.

A total **eclipse** of the sun.

These bright blobs in the sky are called 'sundogs'. They are caused when sunlight is bent by ice crystals high in the atmosphere, producing a bright spot in the sky on either side of the sun.

Total sunblock!

Sometimes the moon moves between Earth and the sun. This blocks the sun's light and causes a solar eclipse. Most eclipses are just partial (they do not cover the sun completely). Occasionally, the moon completely covers the sun for a few minutes, causing a total eclipse. During a total eclipse, the sky goes dark, bright stars and planets are clear and the edge of the sun can still be seen around the dark moon.

Light fantastic

Aurorae are fantastic, multicoloured lightshows that appear in Earth's atmosphere. They are caused by particles from sun meeting with the Earth's magnetic field. Aurorae are best seen from **polar areas** because the winds from the sun travel along the magnetic fields above Earth's **poles** and cause gases high in the atmosphere to glow. Large aurorae can sometimes be seen from as far south as Florida!

This bright green aurora was seen in the skies above western Iceland.

MERCURY

Mercury is the planet closest to the sun. It orbits the sun incredibly quickly, making four complete journeys around it every year. As Mercury is so close to the sun, it never moves far from its glare. It moves so quickly that it can only be seen from Earth six times a year, for two weeks at a time. During these times, it is only visible before sunrise or after sunset.

Smallest planet

Mercury is the smallest of all the planets. It has a very thin atmosphere and has no weather at all. With no atmosphere to spread the heat around the planet, there is a huge difference in temperature between its day and night sides. Its sun-facing day side becomes as hot as an oven at its highest setting, while its night side plunges to around twice as cold as the coldest temperature ever recorded on Earth.

Mercury, ⟹ photographed by the Mariner 10 space **probe**.

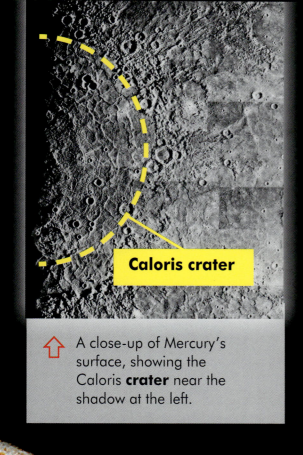

Caloris crater

⇧ A close-up of Mercury's surface, showing the Caloris **crater** near the shadow at the left.

Enormous crater

Packed with craters, Mercury's rocky surface looks a lot like the moon. The craters were caused by asteroid impacts – city-sized chunks of rock that smashed into the planet's surface. Most of Mercury's craters were made many billions of years ago, shortly after the solar system formed. The planet's biggest crater is a giant scar that was caused by an asteroid. It is called Caloris Basin and the whole of Kansas, USA, could fit inside it!

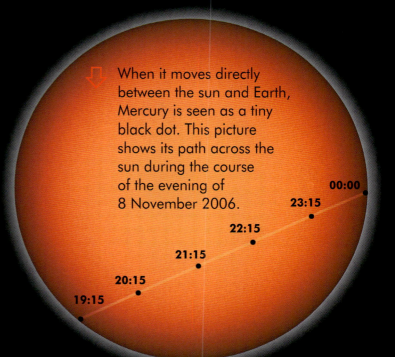

⇩ When it moves directly between the sun and Earth, Mercury is seen as a tiny black dot. This picture shows its path across the sun during the course of the evening of 8 November 2006.

00:00
23:15
22:15
21:15
20:15
19:15

Amazing

Rare sightings

On rare occasions, Mercury moves directly between the sun and Earth, when it can be seen through a telescope for just four hours as a black silhouette. The next time Mercury can be seen in this way will be on 9 May 2016.

VENUS

Venus is the second planet from the sun and is nearly as big as Earth. The Romans named Venus after their goddess of love because it is such a bright and beautiful planet. In fact, it is so bright that it is easy to see in the sky and has even been mistaken for a UFO!

Seeing with radar

Venus is covered with a very cloudy atmosphere. This reflects a lot of sunlight back into space and is what makes the planet so bright. Its atmosphere also stops heat from escaping – the surface temperature on Venus is 467°C. Although clouds hide its surface, scientists have been able to see through with space-probe **radars**.

⬆ A view of Venus through a telescope.

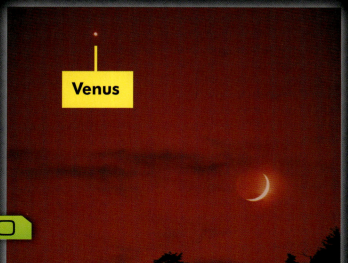

Venus

⬅ Venus and the moon can be seen shining brightly in the evening sky.

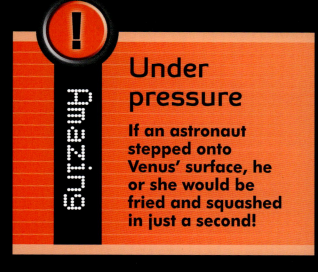

Under pressure

If an astronaut stepped onto Venus' surface, he or she would be fried and squashed in just a second!

Probing for information

Several probes have landed on Venus and taken pictures. The planet's surface is blisteringly hot and the pressure of its atmosphere is enormous – equal to the water pressure 1000 m below sea level! As a result, the probes did not survive for long.

Mountainous landscape

Most of Venus is covered by huge, rolling plains. From these rise a few large **continent**-sized regions, topped with enormous mountain ranges. Venus's highest mountain, Maxwell Montes, is more than 3 km taller than Mount Everest, Earth's highest peak. The planet's largest continent is called Aphrodite Terra and is about the same size as Africa. Any asteroid craters that might have existed on Venus have been worn away by its atmosphere and volcanic eruptions in the past. Venus may still have active volcanoes today.

Beneath its clouds, Venus has a wonderful landscape of rolling plains, volcanoes and mountains.

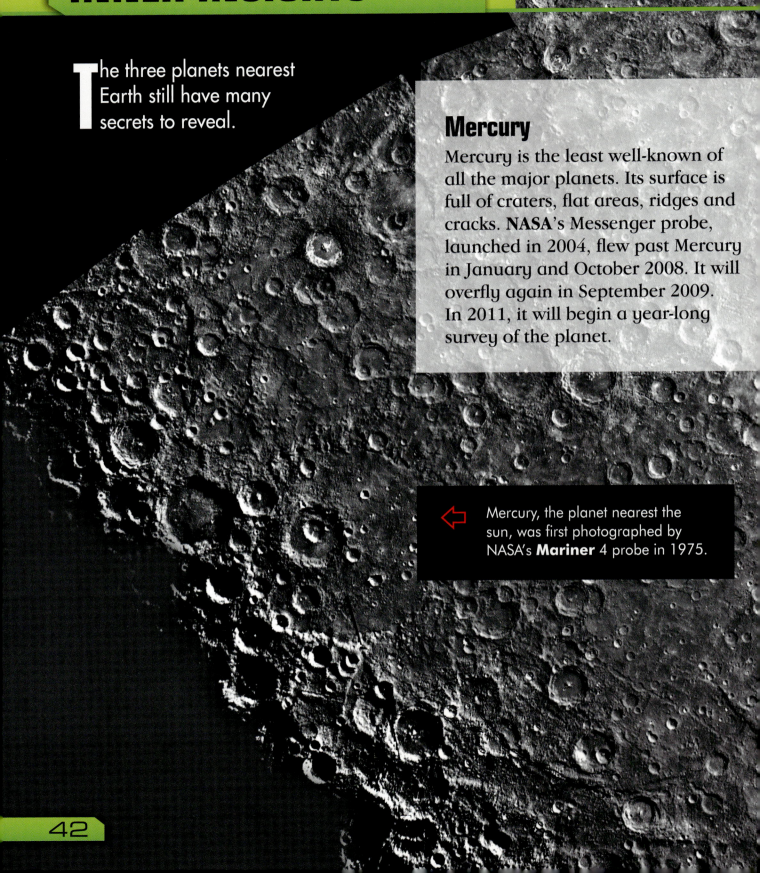

INNER INSIGHTS

The three planets nearest Earth still have many secrets to reveal.

Mercury

Mercury is the least well-known of all the major planets. Its surface is full of craters, flat areas, ridges and cracks. **NASA**'s Messenger probe, launched in 2004, flew past Mercury in January and October 2008. It will overfly again in September 2009. In 2011, it will begin a year-long survey of the planet.

Mercury, the planet nearest the sun, was first photographed by NASA's **Mariner** 4 probe in 1975.

Venus

The surface of Venus, the second planet from the sun, is hidden by its thick, cloudy atmosphere. In 1962, NASA's Mariner 2 became the first successful probe to reach Venus from Earth. The journey took three and a half months. It revealed that the planet's surface is incredibly hot. During the early 1990s, NASA's Magellan probe mapped Venus' surface.

Most of Venus is covered by smooth, hilly areas, from which rise three huge, mountainous **continents**. These are named Ishtar Terra, Lada Terra and Aphrodite Terra. The largest, Aphrodite Terra, stretches halfway around the planet. It is split by an enormous valley called Diana Chasma. In places, the valley is 280 km wide and 4 km deep.

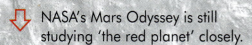
NASA's Mars Odyssey is still studying 'the red planet' closely.

Mighty Maxwell

Rising above the continent Ishtar, Venus' Mount Maxwell is 11 km high. This is much higher than Mount Everest, which at 8.85 km is the tallest mountain on Earth.

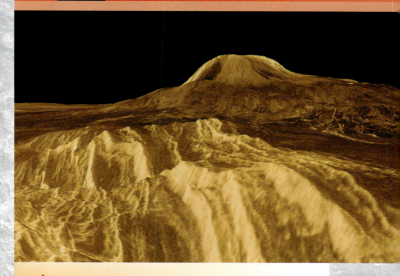

⇧ The Magellan probe took this picture of Venus's mighty Mount Maxwell.

Mars

It takes almost a year to reach Mars from Earth. Mariner 9 was the first probe to map Mars from orbit. It discovered that one side of the planet is heavily cratered, and that the other side is smoother, with some large volcanoes and one huge valley. Mars has been photographed by NASA's **Viking Orbiters**, Mars Global Surveyor and the space probe Mars Odyssey. A European Space Agency probe, Mars Express, has also studied 'the red planet' in great detail.

EARTH AND MOON

Planet Earth is the largest of the four inner planets. Along with its **satellite**, the moon, it orbits the sun once a year. The surface of Earth is called the crust and is a thin layer of rock. It includes the continents and the ocean floor. Beneath Earth's surface, it is so hot that in places solid rock melts into a flowing liquid called **magma**. Magma continually churns beneath Earth's surface and pushes on the solid crust above it.

Moving plates

Earth's crust is a patchwork of large **plates**, which slowly move against each other. When the plates collide with each other, they crumple. This pushes Earth's surface upwards to create a mountain range, such as the Himalayas. Where thin ocean crust is forced beneath thicker continental crust, the rocks melt deep inside the hot magma. This melted rock may later rises like a bubble into the crust above. Volcanoes occur where it breaks through Earth's surface.

Earth seems to be a giant jigsaw when its plates are drawn on a map.

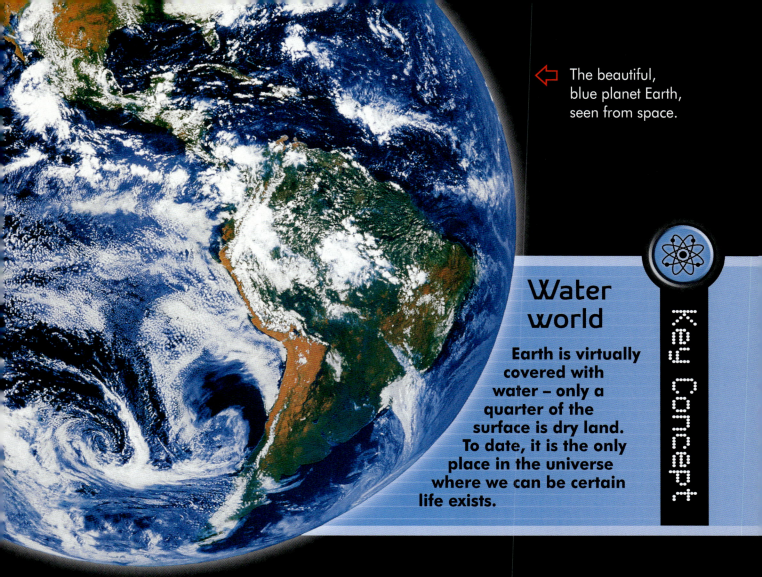

The beautiful, blue planet Earth, seen from space.

The moon

The moon is almost as wide as the USA. It orbits Earth once a month. No wind ever blows there, no clouds ever appear in its skies and no water ever quenches its dry surface. Life never developed on the moon. Some parts of the moon's surface are covered with asteroid craters. There are also many large plains of dark solidified **lava,** once thought to be seas.

Earth's moon is a lifeless place, covered in asteroid craters.

Mars is just over half the size of Earth and is the fourth planet from the sun. It takes nearly two years to orbit the sun. Every few years, Mars appears particularly bright for a month or two in the midnight sky, when it is at its closest point to Earth. Believing the planet looked like a drop of blood, the Romans named it Mars after their god of war. Its red colour is due to the rust in its **iron**-rich soil. Mars has two moons, Phobos and Deimos.

Mars, viewed by the Mars Global Surveyor.

Mariner Valley

Amazing

Martians!

Astronomers in the 19th and early 20th centuries imagined they had seen a network of straight lines on Mars. Some claimed they might be canals **built by intelligent Martians!**

Cold, dusty planet

Mars is very cold. It has just a thin atmosphere in which we would not be able to breathe. However, of all the planets in the solar system, Mars is the most similar to Earth. A day on Mars is just a little longer than our own day. The planet also has its own seasons.

Rocky deserts and dust **dunes** spread across Mars, and its poles are covered with ice caps. Mars has **canyons**, such as the Mariner Valley. It also has **gullies**, which show that large amounts of water may once have flowed across its surface when the planet was a lot warmer and wetter than it is today.

⇧ Mount Olympus is a giant extinct volcano that towers above the plains of Mars.

Life on Mars?

It is possible that **primitive** life may have existed on Mars a long time ago. In August 1996, **NASA** claimed it had discovered traces of **fossil bacteria** in a **meteorite** from Mars. There may even be life on Mars today, hidden in its red soil.

⇦ NASA has landed several probes on the surface of Mars, including two robotic, wheeled rovers called Spirit (left) and Opportunity. These two probes discovered that certain rocks and minerals on the planet had formed in water, proving that there was once water on Mars.

ASTEROIDS AND DWARF PLANETS

In the 18th century, astronomers discovered a gap in space between Mars and Jupiter. Believing a mysterious planet existed there, they formed a group to search for it. The group was called the 'Celestial Police'. On 1st January 1800, astronomer Giuseppe Piazzi spotted a faint object slowly orbiting the sun between Mars and Jupiter. It was so small that it simply looked like a point of light, so it was said to be a '**minor planet**' or asteroid. It was later named Ceres.

As wide as Texas, Ceres is the biggest object in the asteroid belt.

Minor planets

Ceres turned out to be just one of thousands of minor planets orbiting the sun in what we now call the **asteroid belt**, between Mars and Jupiter. Over 400,000 minor planets have been found to date.

Asteroid zone

Asteroids are chunks of rock that formed during the early days of the solar system. Groups of asteroids orbit in front of and behind Jupiter. Thousands of Asteroid-like objects have been discovered orbiting neptune.

Large chunks of rock, called meteors, sometimes blaze through our skies and hit Earth's surface, causing craters.

Smashing rocks

Small asteroid chips, called meteorites, sometimes land on Earth. Chunks of asteroid can blast out craters in Earth's crust. 65 million years ago, an asteroid impact is thought to have wiped out the dinosaurs. Some asteroids burn up in the Earth's atmosphere, when we call them 'shooting stars' or meteors.

asteroid

The first dwarf planets

At 1000 km wide, Ceres is the largest object in the Asteroid Belt. In 2006, Ceres was upgraded from an ordinary asteroid to a dwarf planet. At the same meeting, it was decided to downgrade Pluto from a regular planet (something it had been considered to be since its discovery in 1930) to a dwarf planet. Measuring just 2390 km across, Pluto was thought to be too small to be a major planet. Another dwarf planet named Eris, slightly larger than Pluto, was discovered in 2003.

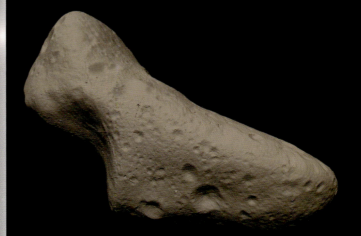

The asteroid Eros is a strangely shaped chunk of rock that is about as big as the island of Manhattan, in New York, USA.

49

Between the planets Mars and Jupiter lies the asteroid belt. This broad zone contains tens of thousands of huge space rocks – material left over from when the solar system was formed. Asteroids are tens of thousands of miles apart from each other.

Visiting probes

In the 1990s, NASA's Galileo space probe photographed three asteroids. One was Gaspra, an angular mountain of rock about 18 km long. Another was Ida, a potato-shaped asteroid that is 50 km long. The third was Dactyl, a tiny asteroid in orbit around Ida. In 1997, NASA's NEAR-Shoemaker probe photographed an asteroid named Mathilde. In 2001, it orbited around an asteroid named Eros. It ended its mission by making a bumpy landing on Eros's surface.

⇧ The icy nucleus of Halley's Comet was viewed by the Giotto space probe.

More missions

Japan's Hayabusa probe took detailed images of asteroid Itokawa in 2005. In 2010, it will bring back samples of dust collected from the asteroid's surface. NASA's Dawn Mission will study asteroid Vesta between 2011 and 2015.

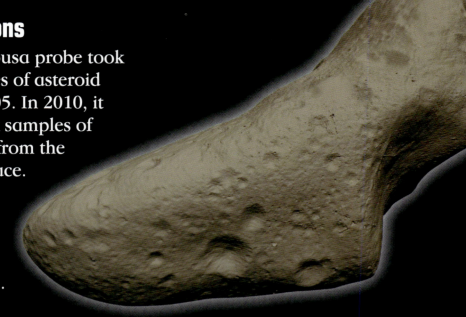

The NEAR-Shoemaker probe eventually landed on asteroid Eros. Eros is 30 km long, and curvy in shape.

Cool comets

Comets are huge lumps of ice and rock. As they near the sun, their surface heats up and the ice turns to gas, freeing the dust that was trapped inside. The center of the comet, known as a nucleus, becomes surrounded by a hazy cloud called a coma, and a long tail of gas and dust streams away from it.

NASA's Stardust space probe took this image of Comet Wild 2 in 2004.

Halley's Comet

Halley's Comet has been seen and recorded by people on Earth for more than 2,000 years. It made its last passage through the solar system in 1985–86. A European probe named Giotto sped into Halley's coma and photographed its nucleus at close range.

Several other comets have been visited by probes. In 2004, NASA's Stardust probe collected material from the coma of Comet Wild 2 and returned it to Earth to be studied.

JUPITER

upiter is the solar system's biggest planet. It is so large that more than a thousand Earths could fit inside it! It is made up mainly of hydrogen and helium gas.

Ball of gas

Jupiter spins on its **axis** once every ten hours – so fast that it bulges out at its centre. Its cloudy atmosphere has light- and dark-coloured streaks, amazing cloud patterns and spots. In Jupiter's atmosphere, a storm rages that is larger than Earth! It is called the Great Red Spot and may have swirled around Jupiter's atmosphere for more than 350 years. As Jupiter is a ball of gas, it does not have a solid surface that a space probe could land on. At the planet's centre, there may be a core of **molten rock** bigger than Earth.

Jupiter's moons

Jupiter has more than 60 moons. The two largest moons, Ganymede and Callisto, are bigger than the planet Mercury. Io is bigger than our own moon and is covered in active volcanoes. Europa is a little smaller. Scientists think that beneath its icy surface, there may be an ocean of warm, salty water in which primitive sea life has developed.

Europa

Ganymede

Callisto

Io

Great Red Spot

Project

Viewing Jupiter and its moons

Use a good astronomy **magazine to find the position of Jupiter in the night sky. Then, look at the planet through binoculars. You will probably see a small, bright oval with several dimmer points of light near to it. If you do a drawing that shows the position of these points of light, and do the same again the following night, you will find that they have moved. These are Jupiter's moons.**

⇧ Jupiter's Great Red Spot can be seen on its surface.

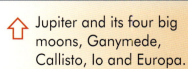

⇧ Jupiter and its four big moons, Ganymede, Callisto, Io and Europa.

SATURN

Saturn is the solar system's second-biggest planet. A ball of mainly hydrogen and helium gas, like Jupiter, it bulges outwards at its centre because it spins so quickly on its axis. It is the least **dense** of all the planets – if it was shrunk to the size of your fist, it would weigh less than a snowball!

Windy planet

Saturn's atmosphere has a few streaky clouds, but it is a very stormy planet. Saturn has very high winds, which can reach speeds of up to 1170 km per hour. That's five times faster than the strongest hurricanes on Earth!

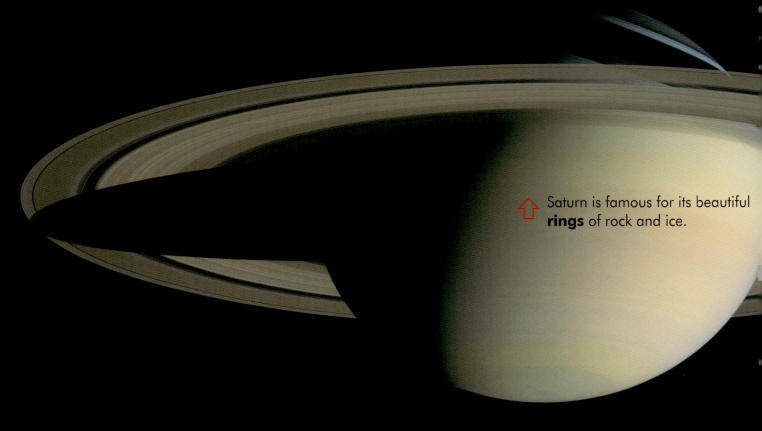

⇧ Saturn is famous for its beautiful **rings** of rock and ice.

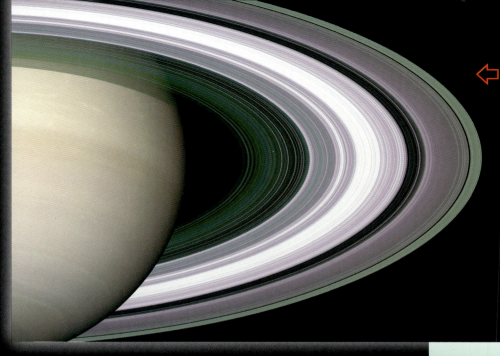

Saturn's system of rings is one of the solar system's most beautiful sights. This close-up view by the Cassini probe shows that the rings are made up of hundreds of narrow bands.

Rings of rock and ice

From a distance, Saturn's rings look like solid, flattened hoops. They block out the light from the sun to cast dark shadows onto the planet below. The rings are made up of millions of small chunks of rock and ice. Viewed from Earth over the years, the rings appear to open up, close, and open up once more. This is caused by the changing tilt of Saturn as it orbits the sun.

Saturn's moons

Around 60 large moons orbit Saturn. One of them, Titan, is a true giant. Bigger than the planet Mercury, Titan is the only satellite in the solar system that has its own atmosphere. Titan has an icy landscape of hills and volcanoes. It may also have rivers and lakes made up of a **chemical** called methane.

Titan, Saturn's biggest moon. Titan has a yellow surface made of nitrogen and **methane gas**. The yellow surface is hidden behind a veil of blue-green cloud.

OUTWARD BOUND

Sending space probes beyond the asteroid belt and into the far reaches of the solar system is a difficult task. They must be launched at the right time, at just the right speed, and in exactly the right direction so that they can eventually meet a planet hundreds of millions of miles away, at a time years in the future!

Key Concept

Probing space

Space probes use their engines to make small adjustments to their speed and direction. To make big changes, they use the gravity of other planets. Complicated mathematics and powerful computers are used by mission controllers on Earth to make each probe's movements as precise as possible.

On Jupiter's surface is a large red oval called the Great Red Spot. It is a storm that has been raging in Jupiter's atmosphere for centuries.

Great Red Spot

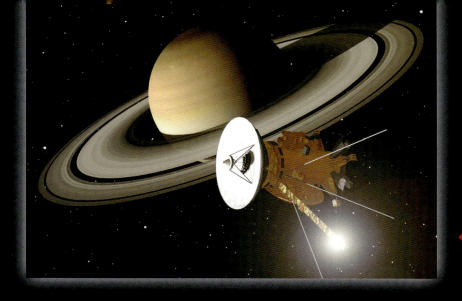

NASA's Cassini space probe investigated Saturn, its rings and its many moons.

Pioneer

Pioneer 10 was the first spacecraft to cross the asteroid belt. It encountered the giant planet, Jupiter, in December 1973. Pioneer 11 reached Jupiter a year later. It went on to fly past the ringed planet, Saturn, in September 1979.

Voyager

Voyager 1 has been travelling in space since it was launched in September 1977, making it the longest-lived space probe. It photographed the planet Jupiter in 1979 and the planet Saturn in 1980. Voyager 2 soon followed, and it took the first (and, so far, only) close-up photographs of Uranus in 1986 and Neptune in 1989.

The images sent back by the Voyager probe show the clouds in the atmospheres of the outer planets as dark belts, bright zones, spots, ovals and swirls. Hot, active volcanoes were discovered on Jupiter's innermost moon, Io, and cold fountains of **liquid nitrogen** on Neptune's moon, Triton. The probes also showed us craters on most of the moons and other features such as mountains and valleys.

Voyager's images of the outer planets and their satellites are amazingly sharp and colourful. The most distant planet, big blue Neptune, was imaged by Voyager 2 in 1989.

URANUS AND NEPTUNE

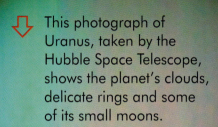

This photograph of Uranus, taken by the Hubble Space Telescope, shows the planet's clouds, delicate rings and some of its small moons.

moons

Of the eight planets in our solar system, Uranus and Neptune are farthest from the sun. Uranus takes more than a human lifetime to orbit the sun. It is green-blue in colour and four times wider than Earth. It was the first planet to be discovered using a telescope. Until then, only Mercury, Venus, Mars, Jupiter and Saturn were known (the only planets visible to the naked eye). Uranus has many satellites or moons. The biggest is Titania, which is made of ice and rock.

Mysterious planet

During the early 19th century, astronomers discovered that Uranus took an unusual path around the sun. This could only be caused by another unknown planet, farther out in space, tugging on it and so changing its orbit. In 1846, this mysterious planet was seen for the first time and named Neptune, after the Roman god of the sea.

William Herschel (1738–1822) discovers Uranus

On 13 March, 1781, amateur astronomer William Herschel spotted a small circular object that didn't look like a star or comet. It was a mysterious new planet that lay far beyond Saturn. Saturn is the Roman name for the Greek god Cronus. The new planet was named Uranus, in honour of Cronus's father.

William Herschel. The ⬆ chart he is holding shows his discovery of Uranus.

Neptune

Neptune is the most distant planet in our solar system. Its orbit takes it 30 times farther from the sun than Earth's. On 29 May, 2011 Neptune will have made just one circuit around the sun since its discovery in 1846.

Even though Neptune is in distant, freezing space, a lot of activity takes place there. Storms often well up in the planet's cloud belts, blown by the strongest winds in the solar system.

Neptune's biggest moon, Triton, is a frozen world with active volcanoes that spurt out icy gases and dust.

This picture of ➡ Neptune was taken by the Voyager 2 space probe in 1987.

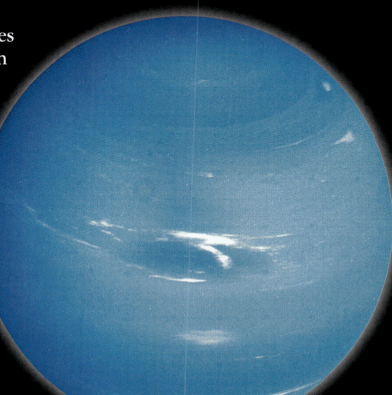

PLUTO, ERIS AND THE KUIPER BELT

When tiny, distant Pluto was discovered in 1930, it was initially declared the solar system's ninth planet. Pluto's orbit takes it 50 times farther than Earth from the sun and takes almost 250 years to complete! The new horizons space probe, launched in 2006, will take nine years to reach Pluto. Pluto has three moons. The largest, called Charon, is about half the size of Pluto itself. It also has two tiny moons called Nix and Hydra. Even farther from the sun than Pluto is the Oort Cloud, an area of space that scientists believe is filled with comets.

Eris

sun

The Kuiper Belt

Hundreds of big asteroids exist beyond Neptune in a zone called the Kuiper Belt. It was only discovered ten years ago. In 2003, a Kuiper Belt object slightly bigger than Pluto was discovered and named Eris. Astronomers recently decided that both Pluto and Eris should be classed as dwarf planets, because they are not big enough to be major planets. Our solar system now has just eight planets.

 Eris is so far away that the sun looks like a bright star in its skies.

A space probe took this photograph of Halley's Comet and its stunning tail of dust and rock. The comet's surface is icy and covered in craters.

Comets

Comets are mountains of ice, dust and rock, which formed in the deep, frozen areas of the outer solar system. A number of comets travel regularly to the inner solar system. The most famous of these is Halley's Comet, which approaches the sun every 76 years. Many billions of comets may exist in the Oort Cloud.

Pluto's moon, Charon.

Dwarf planet, Pluto.

Comet tails

When a comet approaches the sun, its icy surface heats up and gives off gases. As the ice melts, bits of dust and rock that were trapped in it are freed. They float into space and trail behind the comet, creating an amazing tail.

Key Concept

THE BLUE PLANET

Our planet, Earth, is one of eight planets that make up our solar system. The planets circle a star called the sun. We depend upon the sun's tremendous heat and light to create our weather and help keep us, other animals and plants alive.

Earth is a medium-sized planet, the fifth largest in the solar system. It measures 12,756 km in diameter, so it would take you several years to walk around it.

Our place in the universe

Earth is our home in the vast **universe**. Since the first astronaut blasted off into **space** in April 1961, only 24 people have managed to see our planet from space. There, it appears a beautiful, blue globe spinning through the inky black vastness of space. It is an overwhelming sight.

Our planet, Earth, photographed by ⇧ astronauts returning from the **moon**.

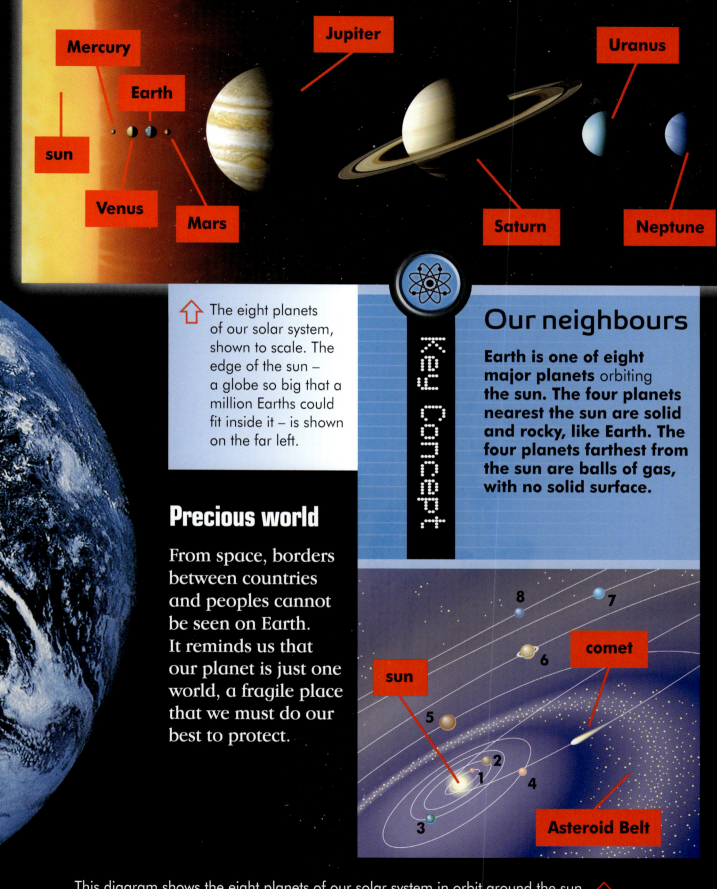

Mercury

Jupiter

Uranus

Earth

sun

Venus

Mars

Saturn

Neptune

⇧ The eight planets of our solar system, shown to scale. The edge of the sun – a globe so big that a million Earths could fit inside it – is shown on the far left.

Key Concept

Our neighbours

Earth is one of eight major planets orbiting the sun. **The four planets nearest the sun are solid and rocky, like Earth. The four planets farthest from the sun are balls of gas, with no solid surface.**

Precious world

From space, borders between countries and peoples cannot be seen on Earth. It reminds us that our planet is just one world, a fragile place that we must do our best to protect.

8   7

comet

6

sun

5

2

1   4

3

Asteroid Belt

This diagram shows the eight planets of our solar system in orbit around the sun. (1. Mercury, 2. Venus, 3. Earth, 4. Mars, 5. Jupiter, 6. Saturn, 7. Uranus, 8. Neptune.) The solar system also includes the **Asteroid Belt** and many **comets**.

YOUNG EARTH

More than 4.6 billion years ago, the blast from an exploding star disturbed a cloud of dust and gas. The cloud began to spin and pull together. This is how scientists believe the sun was created. The sun's gravity kept pulling in more material, and this produced planets, lots of moons, and asteroids and comets. This made up the solar system, including our Earth. As Earth grew bigger, its inside got hotter. Soon, it began to melt the metals in its rocks. These metals sank to Earth's centre and formed its core. Lighter material rose to form the planet's outer layer, called its crust. The mantle is a layer of molten rock between the core and crust.

The moon is thought to have been formed when a planet the size of Mars crashed into Earth.

Amazing

A big whack

The moon was formed by a crash. Scientists believe that a planet half the size of ours struck the young Earth, throwing out a massive sheet of melted material. Much of this material was pulled back together by gravity and formed the moon.

Asteroid attack

For more than a billion years after Earth was formed, asteroids frequently smashed through its thin, rocky crust. This allowed hot, melted rock to burst through and spread over the surface as sheets of bubbling **lava**. Over time, these helped to build up Earth's crust.

The moon was also hit by asteroids, which formed **craters** on its surface. If Earth's surface hadn't continued to be changed by the movements of its crust, **volcanoes** and **weathering**, it would have as many craters as the moon.

Both Earth and the moon were hit by many asteroids in their early history.

Lakes and seas

The impact of the asteroids created a lot of heat. Once asteroids started hitting the planet less often, Earth's crust began to cool and thicken. Volcanoes continued to erupt, spewing out lava and releasing water vapour into the air. As Earth cooled, water vapour turned into liquid. Small puddles slowly turned into lakes and seas. Icy comets sometimes hit Earth, too, adding to the water on its surface when they melted. Earth now had areas of land and of water.

We can see craters billions of years old on the surface of the moon. Despite being very old, they look quite new. They have steep walls and sharp rims, and large mountains often rise from their centres.

CONTINENTS, PLATES AND MOUNTAINS

All the landmasses (continents) seen on Earth today were once joined together in a single, giant landmass known as Pangea, which was surrounded by a huge ocean. However, the molten rock of the mantle pushed up on Earth's crust, causing it to break up into smaller pieces, called plates. And as the crust broke into plates, Pangea was split into smaller pieces, too.

Shifting plates

Gaps between the plates became wider as molten **magma** from the mantle pushed into them. This made South America break away from Africa, and India and Australia break away from Antarctica. A hundred million years ago, molten magma also separated Europe from North America. Ocean water filled the space between these new continents, creating new seas and oceans.

North America

Europe

Asia

Africa

South America

Australia

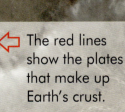

The red lines show the plates that make up Earth's crust.

Alfred Wegener (1880–1930)

We know that the plates of the Earth's crust are moving, and that Earth used to look very different. But how did we find this out? By looking at the shapes of the continents, we can see that they would once have fitted together, like a giant jigsaw puzzle. For instance, if the west coast of Africa was placed next to the east coast of South America, they would fit snugly together. Their rocks and fossils are also similar, suggesting they were once one landmass. The theory that continents move, or drift, was first suggested by German scientist Alfred Wegener, only 100 years ago. Although they move by just a few centimetres each year, over millions of years this adds up to a great distance. We call this moving of continents continental drift.

⇧ The Himalayas is Earth's biggest mountain range – and it's still growing. It was created when India pushed into southern Asia, forcing up Earth's crust.

Mountains

Mountains are formed when two plates push against each other, forcing up Earth's crust. Sometimes, the crust beneath an ocean pushes against the crust beneath a continent. When this happens, the crust beneath the continent is pushed up to make a mountain. The biggest mountain ranges, however, occur when the plates beneath two continents collide and both crumple up.

⇧ Mountains are one of the results of plate movement.

EARTH CHANGES

If Earth could have been seen from space 100 years ago, the shapes and positions of the main areas of land would look the same as those seen today. However, Earth's surface is constantly changing. Some changes happen quickly, such as those caused by earthquakes and volcanoes. Others happen over a longer period of time, such as the wearing away of rocks by weather, water or continental drift.

Parts of Earth's surface are built up when material gathers over a long period of time. This is called sedimentation. The small islands at the mouth of the River Lena, in Russia, were formed in this way. They were made when mud, small bits of rock and other loose material flowed downstream and collected where the river meets the ocean. The islands break up the river into a network of smaller channels, called a delta.

Land shifts

We have only been recording our planet for a few thousand years. This is an incredibly short time compared to the life of Earth. Earth is about 4.6 billion years old. If we could hop into a time machine and zoom through the history of Earth so fast that each century passed in one second, we would be amazed to see mountains being built and wearing away, spaces for oceans being made or squeezed out of existence, coastlines being created and destroyed, and new continents being formed. At the same time, the sea level would rise and fall over time as the **ice caps** at the north and south poles grew or shrank.

Key Concept

Continental drift

Powered by deep movements within Earth's hot mantle, continental drift is still happening. The Atlantic Ocean is widening by about 4 cm each year. India is continuing to collide with south Asia, crumpling the solid crust between the two continents. This is forcing up the mighty Himalayan mountains even farther.

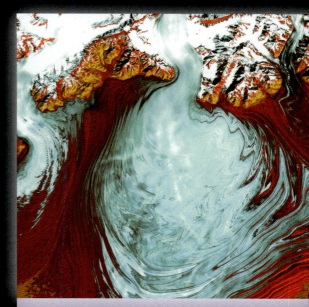

This glacier (part of an ice cap) is slowly melting, as Earth's **climate** warms up. In a few hundred years, the ice may have melted completely. If many glaciers melt, sea levels will rise and flood large areas of land. Earth will look different once again.

This map shows how Europe might look if the sea level rises by 100 m. The lighter blue areas show land that would be flooded.

North Sea

Baltic Sea

antic ean

Black Sea

Mediterranean Sea

VOLCANOES AND EARTHQUAKES

Volcanoes are formed in places where hot, molten rock, known as lava, breaks through Earth's crust and onto its surface. Like mountains, volcanoes are usually found where plates collide or move apart. There are about 1500 active volcanoes around the world. No two volcanoes are exactly alike. Volcanoes around the edges of continents are often tall and steep-sided, built up over the years by eruptions of thick, slow-moving lava and piles of ash.

Vesuvius

One of the most famous volcanoes is Vesuvius, on the west coast of Italy. Vesuvius began as a small, volcanic hill about 25,000 years ago, and it is now 1300 m high. Almost 2000 years ago, an eruption of Vesuvius destroyed the nearby Roman towns of Pompeii and Herculaneum.

In 79 CE, the ancient Roman towns of Pompeii and Herculaneum were completely buried beneath volcanic ash and rock when the volcano Vesuvius erupted. The bodies of victims (like those shown here) were preserved in layers of volcanic ash and can still be seen today.

⇩ This is Mount St. Helens. A mighty mountain peak used to be where the gaping crater is now.

! Amazing

Mount St. Helens

One of the most devastating eruptions of recent times happened in May 1980 in Washington, when Mount St. Helens blew its top. The immense explosion blasted a column of ash into the air up to 25 km high.

Earthquakes

Earthquakes happen when two plates that are locked together suddenly slide apart from each other.

Earthquakes range from mild vibrations to devastating shakings of the ground, which can topple buildings. Small earthquakes happen in Britain each year, but few cause any real damage. Large buildings in areas that suffer from big earthquakes, such as California and Japan, are built to withstand the violent jolting of the ground. Buildings in poorer countries may not be so well made, and great loss of life can occur when an earthquake happens near a big city in which many people live.

Asia

North America

Pacific Ocean

South America

Australia

◻ Ring of Fire

⇧ 90 percent of the world's earthquakes occur along the Pacific Ring of Fire. Here, the plate beneath the ocean is being pushed beneath the surrounding continental plates.

INSIDE EARTH

Earth's natural movements have revealed a lot about the rocks that lie beneath its surface. Layers of rock that were once buried have been lifted up as the crust has moved and shifted. When the Grand Canyon formed, it made a cut in Earth's crust 1600 m deep, uncovering rocks that are more than a billion years old!

Drilling into Earth

Scientists have also been able to learn more about Earth's rocks by drilling into its crust. The USA launched one of the first big scientific drilling projects in 1957. It was called Project Mohole. It drilled through the ocean floor off the coast of Mexico, cutting into the seabed 3 km below the water's surface. The project dug up rocks over five million years old.

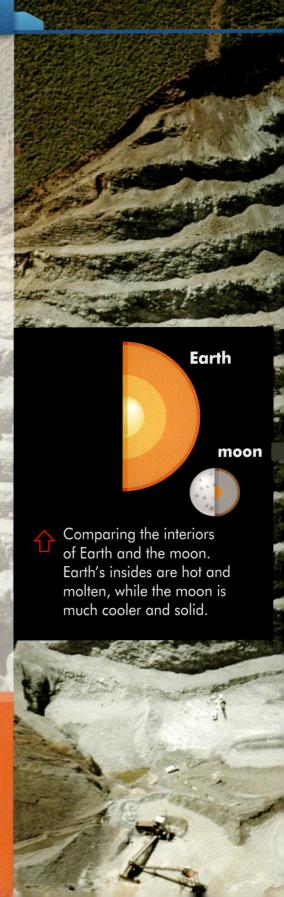

Earth

moon

⇧ Comparing the interiors of Earth and the moon. Earth's insides are hot and molten, while the moon is much cooler and solid.

Amazing

Digging deep

The Kola Superdeep Borehole project in northern Russia has drilled down more than 11 km, and brought up rock samples more than 2.7 billion years old.

Measuring shakes

Incredibly, scientists have learned about the thickness and **density** of Earth's crust, mantle and core by studying the shaking movements caused by earthquakes. Earthquakes cause different kinds of shaking motion – some push and pull the crust, others move it up and down. By measuring these motions, scientists can tell how dense the material is beneath the crust, and so build up a picture of inside our planet.

⇧ Open mines, such as this one in Russia, may look very deep, but they only scratch the surface of Earth's crust.

⇧ A scientific station has been set up on Mount St. Helens to measure the impact of volcanoes and the effects they have on plants and animals.

Three main types of rock make up Earth: igneous rock, sedimentary rock and metamorphic rock.

Igneous rocks

Igneous rocks are formed when molten rock cools and hardens. The igneous rocks formed on Earth's surface are called volcanic rocks. Basalt is a volcanic rock. Pumice is also a volcanic rock, which cooled as it was blasted out of a volcano. It is rough and full of holes caused by the gas bubbles that frothed in it when it was molten.

Igneous rocks formed beneath Earth's surface are called plutonic rocks. They cooled down more slowly than volcanic rocks. Granite is a type of plutonic rock.

Rock hunting

Project

Collect local rock samples and try to identify them. Your local library or museum may have information on the types of rock in your area. Perhaps you are living on an ancient volcano, or on ground that used to be part of the seabed!

⇧ Granite is a plutonic igneous rock made when molten magma cools deep below the ground. It is extremely hard.

This is a sedimentary rock called a conglomerate because it is made up of lots of rock fragments cemented together with a finer material.

Sedimentary rocks

These rocks are the most common type of rocks. Sedimentary rocks, such as sandstone, are formed by the breaking down and weathering of other rocks. Material settling on a seabed can also harden over time to become a sedimentary rock, such as limestone or chalk. These sedimentary rocks are made up of the skeletons of tiny sea creatures. Coal is a sedimentary rock formed from the remains of dead trees and plants.

Metamorphic rocks

Metamorphic rocks are made when one type of rock is changed into a different type by extreme heat and pressure within Earth's crust. Igneous and sedimentary rocks can be changed into metamorphic rocks, and existing metamorphic rocks can be changed into different metamorphic rocks.

Gneiss ('neece') is a type of metamorphic rock.

EARTH AGES

A hundred years ago, **geologists** studying Earth knew that most rocks must be extremely old. For example, a rock such as coal – made from ancient trees and the remains of other plants – needs countless thousands of years of compression beneath Earth's surface to form. However, the geologists could only guess at how old the rocks actually were.

Clocks in rocks

This all changed when scientists discovered 'clocks in rocks'! Geologists found they could measure a special property of the rocks – a property called **radioactivity** – that could tell them how old the rocks actually are.

Geologists use simple hammers to collect rock samples. These samples are then examined in a laboratory with complicated instruments, such as this one, which can measure radioactivity to reveal a rock's age.

A timeline

Geologists have named different periods of time in history to help them date rocks. The oldest rocks are about 4 billion years old, from an age called the Precambrian Period. They are metamorphic rocks from northwest Canada. We know more about conditions on Earth in later periods, from the Cambrian Period (about 540 million years ago) through several more periods to the present Quaternary Period, which began about 1.8 million years ago.

Fossils

Many sedimentary rocks contain fossils. These are impressions of prehistoric life. Some fossilized creatures look like nothing living on Earth today, so they must have died out a very long time ago. Fossils of extinct animals added to the evidence that most of Earth's rocks must be very old indeed.

Most of the fossils we find are millions of years old. This is the fossil of a fish that lived 56 million years ago.

These ancient sedimentary rocks in Arizona, USA, have been worn away by the wind to reveal hundreds of layers.

WATER AND ICE

Three-quarters of Earth's surface is covered with water. This is made up of six major oceans, along with many seas, lakes and rivers. The Pacific Ocean is the biggest ocean in the world. It is 15,000 km wide and 5 km deep – that is much bigger than all the land on Earth put together.

Seas and lakes

Earth has many inland seas and lakes and thousands of rivers. The biggest inland sea is the Mediterranean, which lies between Africa and Europe. The entirely landlocked Caspian Sea is our planet's largest **saltwater** lake, and is in western Asia. The five Great Lakes in North America are the biggest **freshwater** lakes in the world, containing 20 % of Earth's surface freshwater.

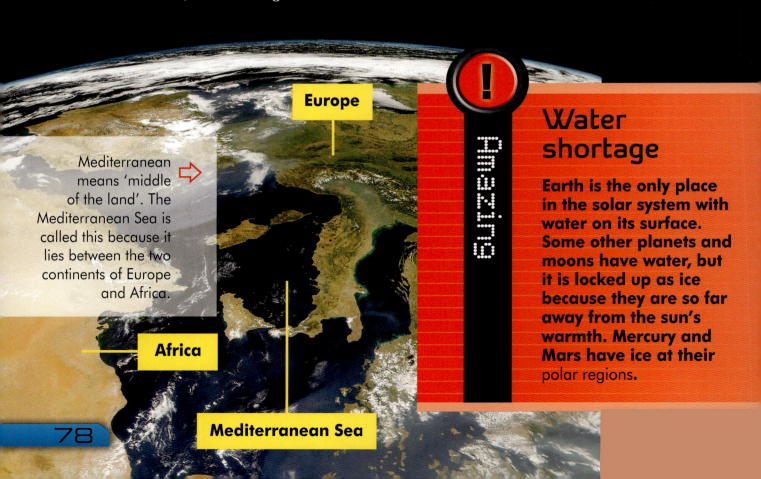

Mediterranean means 'middle of the land'. The Mediterranean Sea is called this because it lies between the two continents of Europe and Africa.

Europe

Africa

Mediterranean Sea

Amazing

Water shortage

Earth is the only place in the solar system with water on its surface. Some other planets and moons have water, but it is locked up as ice because they are so far away from the sun's warmth. Mercury and Mars have ice at their polar regions.

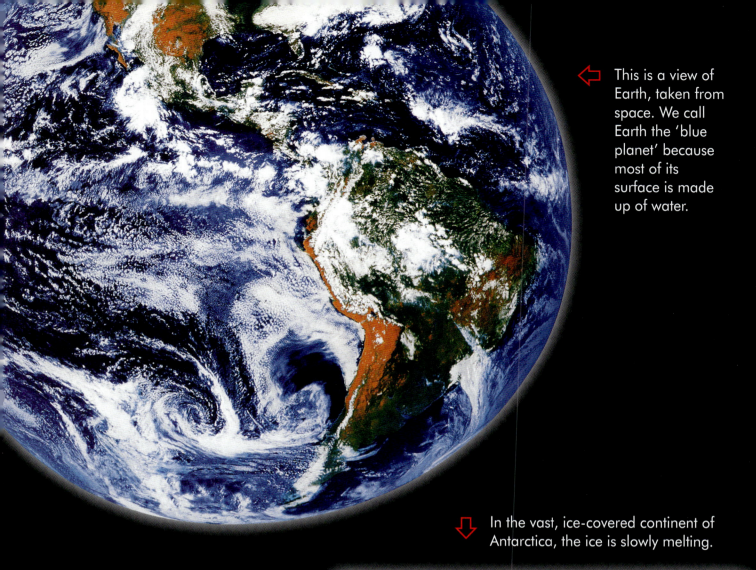

This is a view of Earth, taken from space. We call Earth the 'blue planet' because most of its surface is made up of water.

In the vast, ice-covered continent of Antarctica, the ice is slowly melting.

The icy poles

At the top and bottom of Earth are two areas called the North and South Poles. They are so far from the sun's rays that they are very cold and covered in ice and snow. There have been many times in Earth's history called **Ice Ages**, when Earth has cooled so much that the polar ice has spread farther, covering more land and making sea levels fall. At the moment, Earth is warming slightly, so the ice at the poles is slowly melting and sea levels are rising.

THE ATMOSPHERE

Earth is surrounded by a protective layer of gases, known as the atmosphere. These gases include nitrogen and also oxygen, the gas all life needs in order to survive. The atmosphere contains less of these gases the higher you go. At around 100 km high, there is no more atmosphere, and space begins.

A protective shield

The atmosphere is a barrier that protects us from harm from space. It absorbs dangerous rays from the sun. Most **meteoroids** and small comets from space break up when they enter the atmosphere, but about 500 very small meteorites do reach the Earth's surface every year.

 Are more severe **hurricanes** a result of **global warming**? This picture is of Hurricane Andrew approaching the southern coast of the USA, in August 1992.

A climate blanket

Most of the atmosphere is contained within a layer 10 km deep. Heat and water vapour move around the Earth inside the atmosphere, giving us our different weather and climate patterns.

Key concept

Displays in the atmosphere

Some wonderful sights in the night sky are produced in the atmosphere. Bright flashes of light, called **meteors**, are caused when tiny bits of comet burn up in the atmosphere. Most meteorites are small, harmless chunks of meteoroids. When they travel through Earth's atmosphere they become spectacular fireballs.

⇧ When small objects from space, such as these meteorites, enter the atmosphere, they burn up and leave a trail behind them.

⇦ The aurorae are multicoloured light displays that take place in the atmosphere. They are caused when particles from the sun interact with the Earth's magnetic field, enter its atmosphere, and glow brightly. This is a picture of the Aurora Borealis (Northern Lights), seen over Iceland.

Global warming

Extremes of weather, such as droughts and hurricanes, are sometimes explained as the result of our changing climate, as Earth warms up. Many people think that this global warming has been caused by human activity. Our cars, planes and factories release too many harmful gases into the atmosphere, damaging it so that it cannot protect us so well. We need to look after our atmosphere so that it can continue to do its job.

LIFE ON EARTH

As we have seen, planet Earth is special in many ways. Perhaps its most special quality is that it is a planet upon which many different plants and animals can survive.

Life begins

Life first appeared on our planet about 3.5 billion years ago. Simple life was able to change carbon dioxide gas and water into oxygen. Other life forms then developed that made use of this oxygen. About 540 million years ago, at the beginning of the Cambrian Period, the life forms on Earth became more complex and varied, and many different plants and animals began to thrive in the sea and on land.

⇩ These thick chalk cliffs are made of the skeletons of countl billions of tiny mar life forms, which lived more than 10 million years ago.

⇧ This is how Earth may have looked at the beginning of the Cambrian Period, as life on Earth began to flourish.

A suitable environment

There are many different environments on Earth, each with animals and plants that are particularly suited to them. Life can be found almost everywhere, from blisteringly hot volcanic vents in the depths of the ocean to the freezing world of Antarctica.

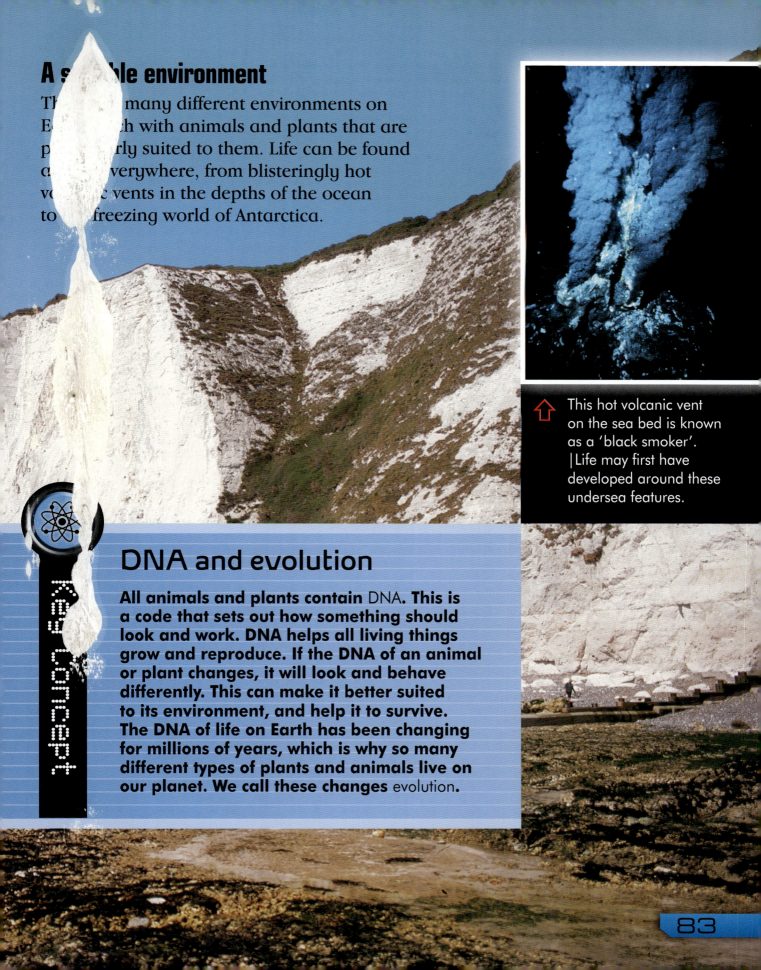

This hot volcanic vent on the sea bed is known as a 'black smoker'. Life may first have developed around these undersea features.

DNA and evolution

All animals and plants contain DNA. **This is a code that sets out how something should look and work. DNA helps all living things grow and reproduce. If the DNA of an animal or plant changes, it will look and behave differently. This can make it better suited to its environment, and help it to survive. The DNA of life on Earth has been changing for millions of years, which is why so many different types of plants and animals live on our planet. We call these changes** evolution**.**

EARTHWATCHING

Satellites allow us to study Earth from space. They have shown us a great deal about its continents, seas, ice sheets and atmosphere. We can also use satellites to watch any changes that affect our planet.

Mapping satellites

Mapping satellites carefully measure shapes on Earth's surface, from the peaks of the Himalayas to the valleys of California. They have also mapped the ocean floors in great detail. Some satellites can even show what types of **mineral** are in Earth's rocks.

At night, satellites show us just how many people live on our planet, when it is lit up with bright city lights, road lights, and industrial fires.

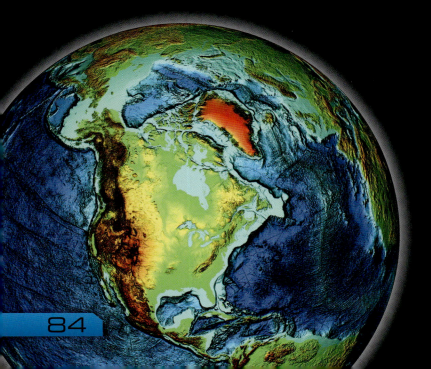

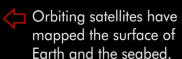
Orbiting satellites have mapped the surface of Earth and the seabed.

Satellite spotting

On a clear night, look up at the sky. If you see a single white point of light, moving slowly in a straight line across the sky, it is probably a satellite. It is orbiting a few hundred kilometres above you. The International Space Station **can also appear very bright because sunlight glints off its large, shiny panels.**

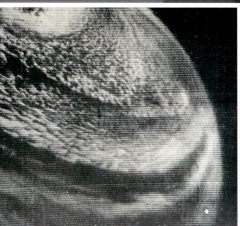

⬆ The first weather satellite image of Earth was taken in 1960.

Weather satellites

Weather was first monitored from space in 1960. Since then, weather satellites have become very advanced. They can now track clouds and storms, identify rain clouds, see the dust blown out into the atmosphere by volcanoes and measure the atmosphere's chemical content.

Humans affecting the planet

Tropical rainforests are cleared every year to make way for land upon which farm animals can feed. In 2006, satellites showed that an area of Brazilian rainforest the size of Greece was destroyed in this way. Changes like this harm plant and animal life, damage our climate and could change the way Earth looks for ever. We must all take better care of Earth so that it continues to be one of the most beautiful and life-filled planets in our solar system.

SKYLAB AND THE SPACE SHUTTLE

After the Apollo missions, America's next space venture focused on a huge space station called **Skylab**.

Skylab

Skylab was a comfortable living and working space for three astronauts. An **observatory** was attached to its upper end, for studying the Sun. Electrical power was provided by **solar panels**. During Skylab's launch, in May 1973, one of its solar panels was torn away. The crew had to repair the damage.

Two more crews visited Skylab after the first crew. The last crew spent three months there, in 1974. NASA had planned to lift Skylab into a higher orbit using its new Space Shuttle. This was never possible, because the Shuttle programme was delayed. Skylab crashed to the Earth in 1979.

Skylab was the USA's first space station.

An amazing machine

The Space Shuttle is the most complicated machine that humans have ever built. It is made up of more than 2.5 million parts, contains 370 km of electrical wiring, and has 27,000 heat-resistant tiles covering its underside.

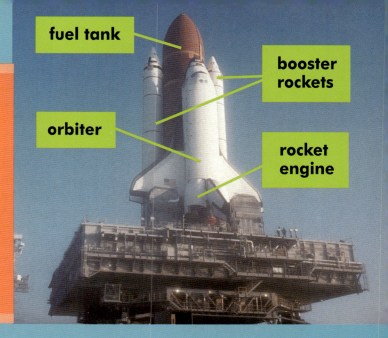

fuel tank

booster rockets

orbiter

rocket engine

Space Shuttle

⬆ Columbia was the first Space Shuttle to blast off into space, in April 1981.

NASA's Space Shuttle is a reusable vehicle lifted into orbit by its own rocket engines and two large rocket **boosters**. Once empty, the boosters fall back to Earth. They are recovered from the ocean and reused. The shuttle orbiter is a vehicle as big as a medium-sized airliner. It can stay in orbit for several weeks, and can carry up to seven astronauts.

Five Space Shuttles were built. Their large cargo bays have often been used to carry a science laboratory called Spacelab, which is used for experiments in space. Many satellites and space probes have also been launched from the cargo bay of the Shuttle, including the Hubble Space Telescope and the Galileo Jupiter probe. Space Shuttles are now being used to take materials and supplies to the ever-growing International Space Station (ISS). They are due to be retired in 2010.

⬅ As it returns to Earth, the Space Shuttle glides down through the air and lands on a runway.

THE INTERNATIONAL SPACE STATION

The International Space Station (ISS) is a large base in which research about space takes place. It orbits Earth and is still being built. It is a joint project between five space agencies including NASA, the Canadian Space Agency, the Russian Federal Space Agency, the Japan Aerospace Exploration Agency and the European Space Agency. It is also the largest programme of scientific cooperation in history, involving 10 countries. So far, the station has been visited by astronauts from 16 nations and the world's first six space tourists.

The Space Shuttle Discovery prepares to dock as it approaches the International Space Station.

The ISS has been growing steadily since 1998, as new **modules**, or parts, have been added. This is how it looked in 2005.

This shows how the International Space Station will look once it is completed.

An ambitious project

Since November 2000, at least two astronauts have been aboard the ISS at any time. It has been kept supplied with food, air, new crew and equipment by manned Soyuz spacecraft and the robotic Progress spacecraft (both from Russia) and by the Space Shuttle. The ISS will be completed by 2010.

When it is completed, the ISS will cover an area the size of a football field. Weighing about 408 tonnes – twice the weight of the Statue of Liberty – the ISS will be the largest structure ever to orbit Earth. Several more modules are due to be added to it. They will give crews of up to seven astronauts as much space to live and work in as the inside of a jumbo jet.

Project

Spot the ISS

The ISS orbits Earth at a height of about 360 km. Each orbit takes just over 90 minutes. This means that, in the right conditions, it can sometimes be seen in the evening sky as a bright, starlike object. Even with binoculars, you will not see more than a bright point of light because it is so far away. You can find out when the ISS will be visible over your location and exactly where to look for it by visiting the Web site www.heavens-above.com.

THE LONELY MOON

The **moon** is Earth's only natural **satellite**. It is a solid ball of rock, about as wide as the United States. Although the moon is our nearest neighbour in **space**, it would take you about six months to reach it from Earth on a nonstop, high-speed train. Astronauts have reached the moon in just three days – but they were hurtling through space at thousands of kilometres per hour.

The moon is 384,400 km) away from Earth – the same distance you would cover if you travelled around the planet 10 times.

Amazing

Bigger than Pluto

Our moon is bigger than the dwarf **planet** Pluto! It is the fourth-biggest moon in the solar system.

The lunar month

The moon takes about a month to make one **orbit** around Earth. It keeps the same side turned towards us, so there is a far side of the moon that we never see.

The moon does not shine – it has no light of its own. Its surface is illuminated by light from the **sun**. In the course of a month, the moon appears to change shape as it orbits Earth in a series of **phases**. At the start of the **lunar** month, the moon looks like a **crescent** in the sky. A week later, the half-moon appears, and after another week, it has become a complete circle. It then narrows to the half-moon again, before becoming a thinning crescent. However, the moon is not actually changing shape. As it orbits Earth, we are just seeing different areas that have come into the sunlight and are being lit up.

 This diagram shows the phases of the moon during the course of a month.

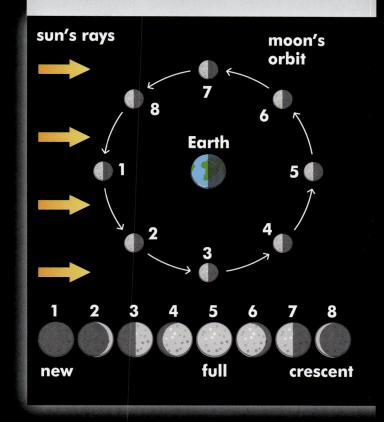

Earthshine

When the moon is a crescent, we may see the rest of it lit with a faint, bluish glow. This is called **earthshine**, and is caused by light being reflected on to the moon from Earth.

 This is a crescent moon, with the rest of the circle faintly lit up by the glow of earthshine.

It was the invention of the telescope, around 400 years ago, that allowed **astronomers** to finally see what the moon's surface was like. The telescope revealed that the moon is a solid, rocky world, with large, grey plains surrounded by **highlands** packed with **craters** and mountains. Astronomers then began to wonder how the moon was originally formed.

The Galileo **probe** took this photograph from above the moon's north pole.

A sister planet?

Some astronomers thought that the moon might be Earth's sister planet, formed from the same cloud of dust and gas that created Earth. Others thought it was so unlike Earth that it must have formed somewhere else in the **solar system** and been pulled towards Earth by Earth's **gravity** when it passed close by.

Today, most astronomers think that the moon was formed around 4.5 billion years ago, when a small planet smashed into young Earth. Large amounts of material from the impacting planet and Earth were thrown into space. Some of this material gathered together in orbit around Earth and became the moon.

Astronomers think a huge crash caused the formation of the moon.

Patchwork moon

Key Concept

The dark patches on the moon are made up of a dark volcanic rock similar to basalt**. On Earth, basalt is spewed out as runny** lava **by erupting volcanoes. The moon's brighter areas are made of rocks containing lighter minerals.**

Moonstuff

The moon is lighter than Earth because Earth has a heavy iron core at its centre, and the moon does not. At the beginning of its life, the moon was very hot. It has since cooled down and, unlike Earth, is now completely solid.

This looks like a photograph of another planet, but it is actually an area of basaltic rock on Earth's surface.

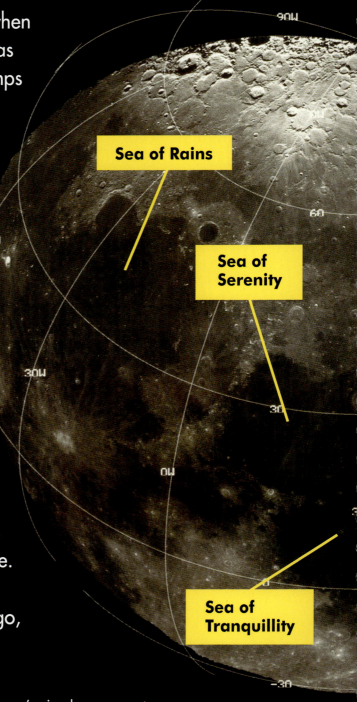

Soon after the moon was formed, when it was still hot inside, its surface was battered by thousands of large lumps of rock called **asteroids**. The biggest of these impacts smashed through the moon's solid, but thin, rocky crust. It carved out gigantic craters and allowed hot, molten rock to pour out onto the surface. These lava flows created the large, dark areas we can see, known as the moon's **seas**. Of course, they are not really seas, but dark lowlands of volcanic lava. They cover a large part of the moon's near side, but only a small part of the far side. This is because the crust on the near side was thinner than the crust on the far side, so it was easier for lava to erupt onto the surface. Eruptions of lava on the moon stopped happening about three billion years ago, and the lava became solid.

Sea of Rains

Sea of Serenity

Sea of Tranquillity

Of all the moon's circular seas, the Sea of Rains is the biggest. It covers an area almost half the size of the Mediterranean Sea.

Sea names

Romantic names have been given to the moon's seas, such as the Sea of Rains, the Sea of Nectar and the Ocean of Storms. At the edges of some seas are bays, such as the Bay of Rainbows and the Bay of Dew. Some dark, inland plains have also been given names, such as the Marsh of Rot and the Marsh of Sleep.

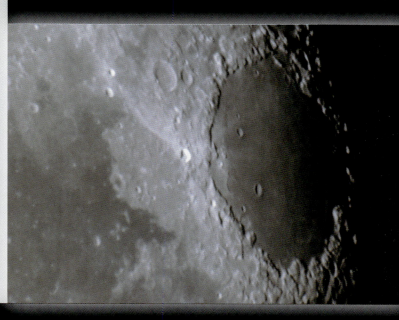

⇧ The Sea of Crises is surrounded by high mountains, seen here from above.

Lunar mountains

Huge mountain ranges surround many of the moon's seas. Some of the mountains in ranges such as the lunar Apennines and the lunar Alps are much bigger than Earth's own Apennines and Alps. Single mountains, or small clusters of mountains, are also found jutting up out of the seas, like islands.

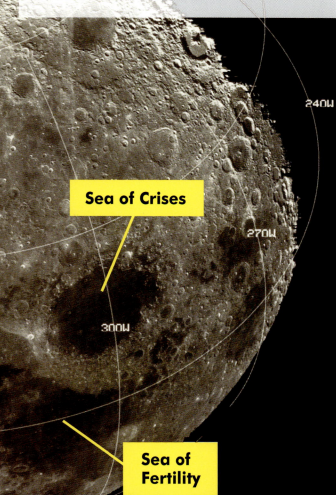

Sea of Crises

Sea of Fertility

The near side of the moon looks different ⇨ from the far side. The near side has more dark 'seas', while the far side (shown here) is covered with craters.

LUNAR CRATERS

The moon's highlands are covered in thousands of craters, or hollows, in the ground. Most of these were formed when asteroids hit the surface of the moon, blasting out masses of solid rock. This happened a very long time ago. Nothing really big has hit the moon for many millions of years.

Endless craters

While most craters look very deep, this is actually an illusion caused by the shadows cast when the sun lights them from a low angle. Most craters are quite shallow compared to their width. If you stood inside a very large lunar crater, you might not even be able to see the walls surrounding you, because they would be beyond your horizon.

This astronaut's-eye view of the large crater Copernicus shows that it is a shallow, bowl-shaped hole in the ground.

Amazing

Giant crater

The biggest crater in the solar system lies on the far side of the moon. It is wider than the dwarf planet Pluto, and is called the 'South Pole-Aitken Basin'. It is so covered with smaller craters, however, that it can hardly be seen on pictures taken by space probes.

Bright ray craters

Some large craters have steep, stepped walls like the seating of a theatre. Many have large mountain peaks at their centre. Bright streaks of material, called **rays,** spread out from many of the moon's largest young craters. This is material that was blasted enormous distances by the impact that formed the crater.

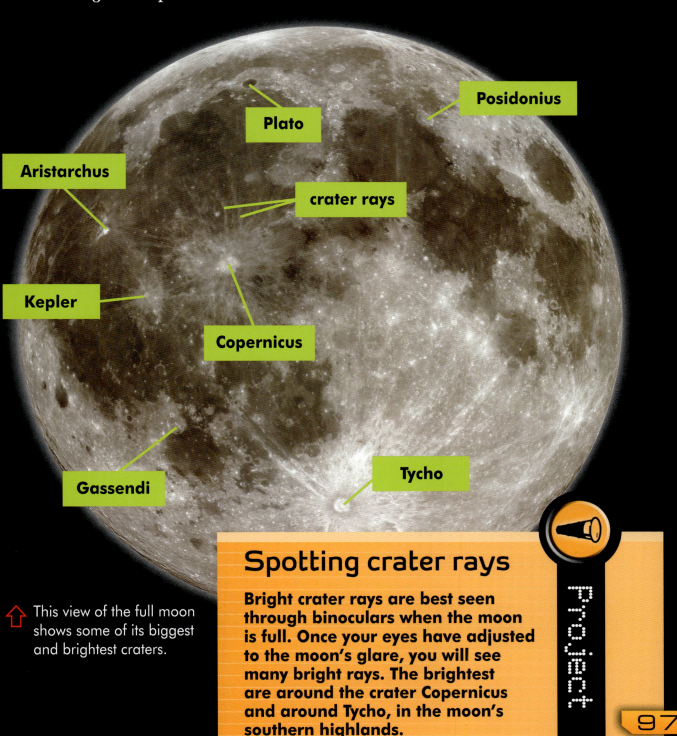

Posidonius

Plato

Aristarchus

crater rays

Kepler

Copernicus

Gassendi

Tycho

⇧ This view of the full moon shows some of its biggest and brightest craters.

Spotting crater rays

Bright crater rays are best seen through binoculars when the moon is full. Once your eyes have adjusted to the moon's glare, you will see many bright rays. The brightest are around the crater Copernicus and around Tycho, in the moon's southern highlands.

Project

CRACKS IN THE CRUST

The moon's crust is made of solid rock. It can stretch a little if it is pulled apart slightly by movement beneath its surface, but after a certain amount of pulling, it cracks. These cracks in its crust are called **faults**, and astronomers have discovered hundreds of them on the moon.

Lunar faults

Most lunar faults are thought to have been made in the moon's early history, after the crust had cooled and the big asteroid impacts and volcanoes had finished sculpting its surface.

The floor of the crater Gassendi is full of **rilles** (see fault valleys opposite). Rilles can be found inside large craters, where they form web-like networks.

Impressive faults

The neatest looking large fault visible on the moon is called the Straight Scarp. Here, part of the Sea of Clouds has been pulled apart to create a cliff that is about 250 m high and 110 km long. Other lunar cliffs caused by faulting are less neat. Some distance from the edge of the Sea of Nectar stands the Altai Scarp – a giant, winding cliff around 500 km long and in places up to 1000 m high.

Fault valleys

In some places, the moon's crust has been pulled apart to produce two faults lying next to each other. Where the crust between the faults has sunk down, a fault valley has been produced. Small fault valleys are known as rilles. Rilles occur around the edges of lunar seas and also cut across highlands and craters.

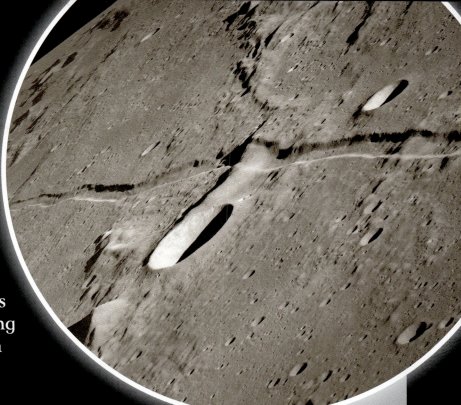

⇧ The Aridaeus Rille on the moon cuts cleanly through all obstacles. It was formed when the moon's crust was pulled slightly apart.

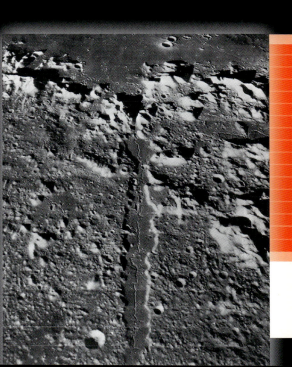

The moon's Grand Canyon

The biggest fault valley on the moon cuts cleanly through the moon's Alps, as if it had been sliced out of the mountains with a gigantic chisel. The Alpine Valley is 150 km long, up to 8 km wide and 2000 m deep.

Amazing

 ⇦ The Lunar Orbiter (one of **NASA**'s space probes) photographed the Alpine Valley.

With binoculars or a small telescope, there is plenty you can see on the moon. These are some of the most impressive features to look at:

1 COPERNICUS Often called the Monarch of the Moon, the crater Copernicus is 93 km across. Its floor is more than 3500 m below its rim. It has a group of central mountains, and is surrounded by bright rays.

2 ARISTARCHUS This is the moon's brightest crater. It is 40 km across, 3000 m deep and its stepped inner walls look like an Ancient Greek **amphitheatre**. A mountain peak rises from the centre.

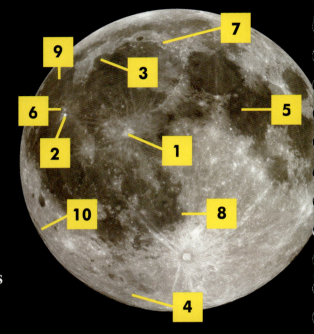

This map shows the locations of the moon's top ten features.

Aristarchus and the nearby Schroeter's Valley.

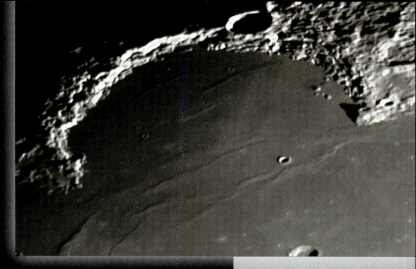

3 THE BAY OF RAINBOWS This beautiful, semicircular bay on the edge of the Sea of Rains is bordered by the magnificent Jura Mountains. One headland of the bay, called Cape Heraclides, looks like the side of a woman's face with long flowing hair behind, so it has been called the Moon Maiden.

⇧ The Bay of Rainbows.

4 WARGENTIN This unusual crater was flooded nearly to the brim with lava, so it looks more like a circular plateau.

5 LAMONT This is a large collection of wrinkles in the Sea of Tranquillity, surrounding a circular formation. When it is lit by a low sun, it looks like a bullet hole in a sheet of glass.

6 SCHROETER'S VALLEY The largest lava valley on the moon is a winding rille, 160 km long and in places 1000 m deep.

7 THE ALPINE VALLEY This fault valley, 180 km long, cuts cleanly through the moon's Alps.

8 THE STRAIGHT SCARP This is the so-called Straight Wall in the Sea of Clouds. It is a cliff caused by faulting in the moon's crust.

9 MOUNT RÜMKER The biggest **dome** on the moon is a long-extinct volcano. It is about 70 km wide.

10 THE EASTERN SEA One of the moon's most spectacular asteroid **impact craters** looks like a giant bulls-eye target. It is made up of a central lava plain, surrounded by rings of mountains and several dark lakes. Overall it measures 1000 km across.

⇦ Mount Rümker.

SOLAR ECLIPSES

An **eclipse** of the sun happens when the moon moves directly between Earth and the sun, blocking its light.

Partial eclipse

In a partial eclipse, only part of the sun is covered by the moon. At first, the curved silhouette of the moon appears at the sun's edge, then it gradually moves across part of its surface. Partial eclipses usually occur several times a year, but they can only be seen from certain parts of Earth's surface. So, in some locations, there may be several years between them.

Total eclipse

Total eclipses are much rarer. They can only be seen from a narrow area of Earth's surface, where the shadow of the moon sweeps across it. The sun is 400 times bigger than the moon, but it is also 400 times farther away, so the two objects look about the same size to us. As the moon can only just cover the whole sun, a total eclipse only lasts for a few minutes.

The sun was completely hidden by the moon in a total solar eclipse in March 2006.

Pearly plumes

During a total solar eclipse, the pearly white plumes of the sun's hot outer atmosphere **can be seen behind the moon, along with the flame-red tongues of gas that jet off the sun's surface.**

⇧ High above the Mediterranean, the crew of the International Space Station photographed the 2006 eclipse, looking at the moon's shadow on Earth.

Eclipse of the moon

Lunar eclipses are less spectacular, but wonderful in their own way. They take place when the moon passes through the shadow cast into space by Earth. For an hour or two, the moon turns a beautiful shade of orange or red, as sunlight is bent around the edge of Earth onto the moon.

 This is a total eclipse of the moon.

There is a limit to how much you can learn about the moon just by observing it from Earth. For centuries, astronomers longed to view its surface up close, to study its far side and to know what it was made of.

Reaching the moon

In September 1959, the Soviet Union (modern day Russia) launched the first probe to reach the moon. A month later, another Soviet probe took the first photographs of the moon's far side. The photos surprised astronomers – the far side had very few dark areas and many craters.

NASA's soft-landing probe ⇧ Surveyor 3 touched down on the moon's Sea of Islands in April 1967.

Ranger, Surveyor and Lunar Orbiter

The United States responded with three very different kinds of robotic moon missions – Ranger, Surveyor and Lunar Orbiter. The Ranger probes were one-way missions: they headed for the lunar surface, taking hundreds of pictures as they closed in, then smashed into the moon at high speed.

The Surveyor probes touched down on the moon and studied the surface in detail. They found that the 'soil' was a few centimetres thick and that it is able to take the weight of a manned lander. Five Lunar Orbiter probes circled the moon, and returned thousands of pictures of its surface.

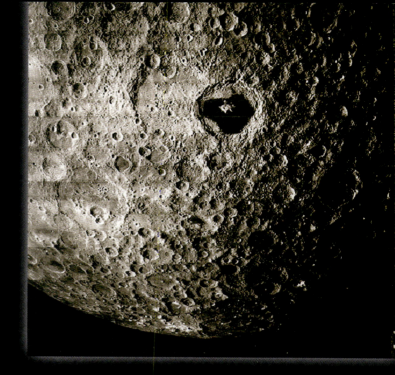

⇧ This picture of the moon's mysterious far side was taken by Lunar Orbiter 3.

Russian probes

Later, Russian probes brought some of the moon's 'soil' back to Earth. In the 1970s, two strange-looking, eight-wheeled robots called Lunokhod crawled around the moon and took hundreds of pictures.

⇩ Ranger 8 took this picture of the southern part of the Sea of Tranquillity, before it crashed into the moon in February 1965.

Space probes

Space probes allow scientists to study the moon from up close. Orbiting probes have mapped the entire moon, while softlanders **have examined small parts of its surface in detail. A few probes have brought samples of the moon's soil and rock back to Earth.**

Key Concept

WALKING ON THE MOON

During the years 1969–1972, the USA's impressive **Apollo** programme successfully landed 12 brave astronauts on the surface of the moon.

Saturn V

Saturn V was the vast rocket that carried the Apollo spacecraft to the moon. It had three stages: the first stage heaved the spacecraft high above the atmosphere, the second stage pushed it into orbit, and the third stage launched it towards the moon.

Apollo 11

In July 1969, Apollo 11 carried astronauts Neil Armstrong, Buzz Aldrin and Michael Collins to the moon. On 20th July, the landing craft Eagle touched down on the Sea of Tranquillity. Armstrong opened the hatch, climbed down the ladder and placed the first human foot on lunar 'soil'. Shortly afterwards, Aldrin followed him. This first lunar walk lasted two and a half hours.

The mighty Saturn V rocket carries Apollo 11 off to the moon in July 1969. In this first stage, its five engines burned 1814 tonnes of fuel in just two and a half minutes.

Biography

First on the moon – Neil Armstrong (1930–2012)

Neil Armstrong learned to fly before he was old enough to drive. He trained as a pilot and became an astronaut with the Gemini Space Programme. **He joined the Apollo Programme and commanded the famous Apollo 11 mission. His words on being the first person to step onto the moon were, 'That's one small step for a man – one giant leap for mankind'.**

⇧ Armstrong, Collins and Aldrin were the crew of Apollo 11. Collins never walked on the moon. He orbited the moon alone in the command module, Columbia.

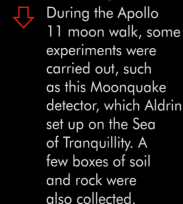

⇩ During the Apollo 11 moon walk, some experiments were carried out, such as this Moonquake detector, which Aldrin set up on the Sea of Tranquillity. A few boxes of soil and rock were also collected.

Apollo 12, Apollo 13 and Apollo 14

Four months later, Apollo 12's landing craft, Intrepid, landed on the Ocean of Storms, near the Surveyor space probe. The astronauts visited Surveyor, which was coated with dust. In 1970, Apollo 13 was cancelled after an explosion, but later that year, Apollo 14's landing craft, Antares, touched down near the crater Fra Mauro. To the amusement of TV viewers on Earth, astronaut Al Shepard whacked a golf ball with a soil sampling stick.

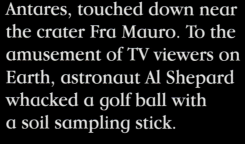

MORE MOON EXPLORATION

An amazing electric moon buggy was used on the final three Apollo missions. It allowed the astronauts to explore areas several miles away from their landing vehicle.

The moon buggy's tyres were made out of piano wire!

Apollo 15

In July 1971, the astronauts of Apollo 15 explored the shoreline of the Sea of Rains. They visited a winding valley called the Hadley Rille, and found a patch of green soil that had been sprayed out of a lava fountain. They showed that objects of different weights fall at the same speed on the airless moon. They dropped a hammer and a falcon's feather from the same height, and both hit the moon's surface at the same time.

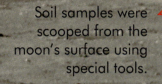

Soil samples were scooped from the moon's surface using special tools.

Apollo 16

A hilly region called the Descartes Highlands was visited by Apollo 16 in April 1972. Using the moon buggy, astronauts explored Stone Mountain and North Ray crater. The crater's inside walls were found to be layered, where ancient lava flows had built up over time.

Apollo 17

Apollo 17, the last mission to the moon, visited an area near the crater Littrow in December 1972. It discovered some bright orange soil, which was later found to be made of tiny coloured beads formed in the intense heat of a meteorite impact.

Soviet space projects

The Soviet Union also had a lunar orbiting and landing programme. They developed techniques useful for a moon landing and they sent unmanned probes to orbit and land on the moon. Their mighty rocket, the N-1, was just as powerful as Saturn V, but it failed disastrously. In the end, their expensive project was abandoned when it became clear that the United States was winning the race to put people on the moon.

Apollo 16 astronaut John Young leaps above the lunar surface as he salutes the US flag.

THE FUTURE MOON

In recent years, several unmanned lunar probes have been sent into space, photographing its surface and mapping it in ever greater detail. NASA's Lunar Reconnaissance Orbiter has even documented the lunar surface in three dimensions! We now know that water ice exists on the Moon's south pole, making it more accessible to human exploration.

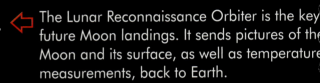

The Lunar Reconnaissance Orbiter is the key future Moon landings. It sends pictures of the Moon and its surface, as well as temperature measurements, back to Earth.

People return to the Moon

It seems certain that humans will set foot on the Moon again before 2025. Although the United States has cancelled its current Moon missions, China is now making plans to explore our mysterious satellite.

The next Moon landing is likely to be similar to the Apollo missions in the 1960s. Astronauts will probably orbit the Moon in a command ship and then land on its surface in a separate vessel.

Once in orbit around the Moon, the astronauts will make their way down to its surface in a four-legged lunar module. They are likely to spend about seven days on the Moon, carrying out experiments, making observations and exploring their surroundings.

All astronauts visiting the Moon in the future will leave behind equipment and supplies that can be used by later missions, as well as material that could be used to make a permanent Moon base.

 Chang'e 2, the last unmanned lunar orbiter from the Chinese Lunar Exploration Programme, was sent to space in this shuttle. Its successor, Chang'e 3, will land on the Moon's surface and take probes to prepare a manned Moon landing.

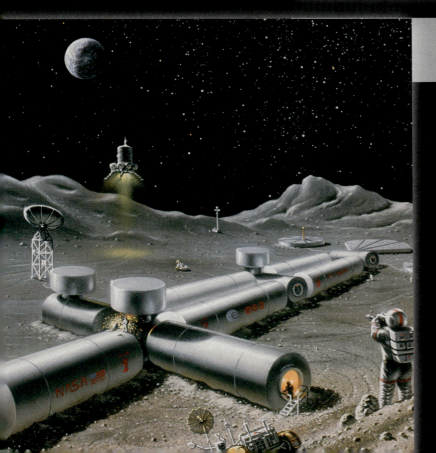

⇐ The first permanent Moon base might look something like this concept by NASA.

Where next?

Our return to the Moon will be a stepping stone for further exploration of the solar system. After the Moon will come the planet Mars. The first human footprint on that distant red planet is likely to be made in your lifetime – perhaps you will be the wearer of the first boot to tread on Mars!

GLOSSARY

Amphitheatre an oval, circular, or semicircular-shaped stadium.

Apollo the USA's manned moon landing programme of the 1960s and 1970s.

Asteroid a lump of rock in space.

Asteroid belt a band of space between Mars and Jupiter in which thousands of large asteroids are found.

Astronaut someone who has travelled more than 98 km above Earth.

Astronomer a scientist who studies space.

Astronomy the scientific study of objects in space.

Atmosphere a mixture of gases found around a star or a planet.

Atom the smallest part of any substance.

Aurorae glowing colours in the night sky made when energy from the sun causes gases in the atmosphere to light up.

Axis an imaginary line between a planet's north and south poles. Planets spin on their axis.

Basalt a dark volcanic rock.

Big Bang the explosion of a single object at the beginning of time, around 14 billion years ago, that created the universe.

Black hole a big star that has died and crumpled in on itself, forming an object with so much gravity that nothing – not even light itself – can escape from it.

Booster the first lift-off stage of a space rocket, or an extra rocket strapped to the side of the main rocket to provide extra thrust.

Canal an artificial waterway.

Canyon a steep-sided valley.

Capsule a small spacecraft.

Chemical a substance that is created when atoms change.

Climate the average temperature and weather experienced in different parts of the world.

Comet a huge lump of frozen gases, ice and rocky debris that orbits the sun. The nucleus of a comet is about the size of a mountain on Earth.

Command module a spacecraft that serves as a central base for astronauts.

Constellation a group of stars within a part of the sky. There are 88 constellations, some of which were formed thousands of years ago.

Continent a large landmass. There are seven continents on Earth: Asia (the largest), Africa, North America, South America, Antarctica, Europe and Oceania (the smallest).

Continental drift the movement of Earth's continents in relation to each other.

Core the heaviest, thickest part of a planet, lying at its centre.

Cosmic a word to describe anything in outer space.

Crater a circular, bowl-shaped hole in a planet's surface. Craters are blasted out by the impact of an asteroid or the explosion of a volcano.

Crescent the shape of the moon at the start and end of a lunar month.

Dense something that is very heavy compared to its volume.

Density how heavy an object is compared with its volume.

DNA the substance in the cells of all plant and animal life on Earth. DNA stands for deoxyribonucleic acid.

Dock the joining together of two spacecraft in space.

Dome a low, rounded lunar volcano.

Dune a wind-blown pile of sand.

Dwarf planet an object orbiting the sun with enough gravity to be a rounded shape, but too small to be considered a proper planet.

Earthquake a shaking motion in Earth's crust caused when two plates slide past each other.

Earthshine the faint, blue-tinted glow of the moon's unlit area, visible with the naked eye when the moon is a narrow crescent. It is caused by sunlight reflected onto the moon by Earth.

Eclipse when the moon moves directly between Earth and the sun, it blocks out the sun's light and causes a solar eclipse. When the moon moves into the shadow of Earth, it produces a lunar eclipse.

Eclipse (solar) when the moon moves between the sun and Earth and it covers the sun's light so that only the edge of the sun can be seen.

Evolution the process by which life forms on Earth have changed to survive in their own particular environment.

Fault a crack in the moon's crust.

Fossil the preserved remains of prehistoric plants and animals in rock.

Fossil bacteria the impression in rock of something that lived long ago.

Freshwater water that does not have much salt. Freshwater is found in most lakes and rivers.

Full moon when the moon appears fully lit up by the sun.

Galaxy a collection of millions, hundreds of millions, or billions of stars, all held together by gravity.

Gas a chemical that is not a liquid or a solid.

Gemini Space Programme NASA's ten manned missions that launched two-person crews into orbit to try out procedures that would be useful in a moon landing.

Geologist someone who studies the structure of Earth's crust and its layers.

Global warming a gradual rise in the average temperature on Earth.

Globular cluster a ball-shaped cluster of very old, red stars containing anything from tens of thousands to millions of stars. Globular clusters are found surrounding galaxies.

Gravity the forces of attraction between all objects with mass in the universe. Gravity is the force that pulls objects towards the Earth. It is also reponsible for keeping the Earth and other planets in their orbits around the sun.

Gullies small water-cut valleys.

Helium a very lightweight gas.

Hemisphere half of Earth. The top half is called the northern hemisphere, the bottom half is known as the southern hemisphere.

Highlands heavily cratered or mountainous areas on the moon. They appear much brighter than the seas.

Hurricane a powerful storm of rain clouds hundreds of miles wide, with average wind speeds over 100 kph.

Hydrogen a very light and colourless gas.

Ice Ages periods of global cooling lasting around 100,000 years, during which the polar ice caps grow.

Ice caps vast, thick sheets of ice covering Earth's polar regions.

Impact crater a pit in the moon's surface formed by an object hitting the moon at high speed.

International Space Station a large structure orbiting Earth in which research about space takes place.

Iron a metal.

Lava hot, melted rock that has bubbled up from below a planet's surface (usually through a volcano).

Light year the distance traveled by light in one year. Light has a speed of 300,000 km per second.

Liquid nitrogen nitrogen gas that has cooled down so much it has become a fluid.

Luna a series of 24 Russian Moon probes launched between 1959 and 1976.

Lunar an adjective describing anything that has to do with the moon.

Magma molten rock beneath a planet's crust.

Magnetic fields areas of magnetic energy.

Mantle a layer of molten rock between Earth's crust and its core, about 2900 km thick.

Mariner a series of 10 probes launched by NASA between 1962 and 1975.

Matter all substances and materials. Everything is made of matter.

Mercury the USA's first space missions with a human crew.

Meteor a strak of light produced as matter in the solar system falls into the Earth's atmosphere. It is also called a 'shooting star'.

Meteorite a small rock that has fallen from space onto Earth.

Meteoroid a small rock in space, usually a chip off an asteroid.

Methane gas a smelly gas.

Milky Way the galaxy that includes our solar system. Under aclear sky, the Milky Way's more distant stars can be seen forming a beautiful misty band.

Mineral a solid material that is found naturally in the ground. Rocks are made out of minerals.

Minor planet an asteroid.

Missile a rocket-powered weapon.

Module a special pod or enclosed compartment that is part of a space station or docked with it as a separate spacecraft.

Molecule a group of atoms. A molecule is the smallest part into which a substance can be divided without changing its chemical nature.

Molten something so hot that it is in a melted state.

Molten rock rock so hot that it is melted and runny.

Moon Earth's only natural satellite. Other natural satellites are also known as moons.

NASA National Aeronautics and Space Administration, the United States' national space agency.

Nebula (plural: nebulae) one of the many glowing clouds of gas or dust in space. Stars are born inside nebulae.

Nuclear reaction a burst of energy caused by atoms hitting each other at high speeds.

Observatory a building where space is studied and scientific information about it is collected.

Open cluster a group of young stars.

Orbit the curved path of a planet or other object around a star, or a moon around a planet.

Parallax when the position of an object seems to change when you look at it from a different place.

Phase the amount by which the moon appears lit up by the sun.

Pioneer a series of 11 probes launched by NASA between 1958 and 1978.

Planet a large, round object that orbits a star. The sun has eight major planets – Mercury, Venus, Earth, Mars, Jupiter, Saturn, Uranus and Neptune.

Plate a large portion of Earth's crust floating on the magma.

Polar areas the regions around a planet's poles.

Poles points at opposite ends of a planet.

Pressure the amount of force applied by one substance on another.

Primitive very simple and undeveloped.

Probe a spacecraft which gathers scientific information.

Program a planned mission to, or in, space.

Pulsar a very heavy rotating object in space that generates regular pulses of radiation.

Radar a sensing system that uses radio waves to detect physical objects.

Radiation all objects in the universe give out radiation, which isany form of energy. For example, heat or light.

Radioactivity energy given off by rocks, which helps scientists to figure out how old the rocks are.

Rays bright lines streaking away from an impact crater across the moon's surface. Rays are made up of material thrown out by the impact that made the crater.

Red giant an old star that has swelled up and cooled down.

Reflector a telescope that uses a mirror shaped like a shallow bowl to collect and focus light.

Refractor a telescope that uses lenses to collect and focus light.

Rille a narrow lunar valley caused by faulting as the moon's crust has pulled apart. They can be straight or curved. Others are winding and snake-like, thought to have been caused by fast-moving lava flows.

Rings large, flat circular hoops made up of dust, rubble, and/ or ice chunks. Rings surround all four gas giants, but are particularly bright and beautiful around Saturn.

Rover an electric-powered wheeled vehicle used to explore other planets and the moon.

Saltwater water that contains a lot of salt. Saltwater is most often found in seas and oceans.

Salyut Russia's space station program.

Satellite a natural or man-made object in orbit around a larger object. Natural satellites are also known as moons.

Seas large plains of basaltic lava on the moon, which look darker than the surrounding areas.

Shenzhou China's human space flight program.

Silhouette a dark, shadowed shape seen against a brighter background.

Skylab a large, 68-tonne space station occupied by three American crews between 1973 and 1974.

Softlanders space probes that gently land upon the surface of the moon or planet.

Solar anything to do with the sun.

Solar panel a device that converts sunlight into electricity.

Solar system an area of space containing our sun, the planets and their moons, asteroids and comets.

Soyuz a series of crewed Russian spacecraft first launched in 1967.

Space everything beyond Earth's atmosphere.

Space Age the era in which we now live, which began in October 1957 with the launch of Sputnik 1, the first artificial, or man-made, satellite.

Space Race the rivalry between the USA and Russia in all areas of space flight and exploration.

Space shuttle a large, reusable winged spacecraft capable of carrying eight crew members into Earth's orbit.

Spacecraft any vehicle that travels in space.

SpaceShipOne the first private spacecraft to enter space.

SpaceShipTwo an eight-seater spacecraft being developed for private space trips.

Star a huge ball of burning hot gas.

Sun our nearest star, a huge ball of burning gas.

Supercluster a gigantic grouping of galaxy clusters, which are all held together by gravity. Superclusters are the biggest objects in the universe.

Supernova the massive explosion of a large, old star.

Surveyor a series of probes that softlanded on the moon between 1966 and 1968.

Telescope an instrument used by astronomers to study objects in space.

Thrust the force of hot gases produced when a rocket burns its fuel.

Universe everything there is, to the unimaginably distant reaches of space.

Venera a series of 16 Soviet probes to Venus launched between 1961 and 1983.

Viking Orbiter NASA's first robotic Mars missions.

Volcano a mountain built up by the eruption of hot, molten rock, and piles of ash.

Vostok Russia's first manned space programme.

Voyager two NASA space probes, launched in 1977, that travelled to the planets of the outer solar system.

Weathering the wearing away of Earth's surface by weather, such as rain and wind.

White dwarf a star about the same size as Earth, made of incredibly dense, tightly packed material.

INDEX